April 8, 1995

To Jo and An

CW00448281

With best wishes

from the author—

John Anthony.

Rook.

GRASPING AT STRAW

GRASPING AT STRAW

John Anthony

The Book Guild Ltd.
Sussex, England

The Book Guild Limited
Temple House
25 High Street
Lewes, Sussex

First published 1992
© John Anthony 1992

Set in Baskerville

Typesetting by Dataset
St Leonards-on-Sea, Sussex

Printed in Great Britain by
Antony Rowe Ltd
Chippenham, Wiltshire

A catalogue record for this book is
available from the British Library

ISBN 0 86332 733 8

1

I sat at a table in this dimly lit smoke-filled pub, 'The George', supping from a pint jug of best bitter. I watched impassively as the heavy drinkers at the bar laughed and joked with increasing volume as they drank the night away.

Suddenly, I was startled by a young lady who had come and sat down at my table. I noticed her badly creased pale pink dress. Hung about her head, in no sense of order, was blonde hair which seemed to cover most of her face. I pretended to ignore her and continued to gaze at the bar until I noticed, out of the corner of my eye, that her left hand, palm down, was pushing its way across the table top towards me. Her hand stopped. I turned and tried to look at her between her blonde curtains of hair. She looked up at me with sad, pleading eyes and lifted her hand to reveal four tablets and muttered, 'Blues'.

I knew 'blues' were used to make people feel high, ecstatically happy and carefree. However, a few hours after taking the pills, a dull, depressing lethargic mood would set in, with a longing for more tablets. I had enough problems of my own without compounding them with 'blues'.

'What is your name?' I said.

'Jill,' came a feeble reply.

I knew she would also sell her body and probably the pink dress, but I said reluctantly, 'No thank you, Jill, but I'll get you a drink.'

I got her a vodka and tonic, which she grasped with her pale wasted hand and politely smiled as if to say that her efforts had not been totally in vain.

Just at that moment there was a banging noise and yelling from the pub corridor near the bar. I looked round and there was Mary-Anne, this tall, curly-haired, pretty part-time opera singer, in hysterics in the corridor while various men were clearly locked outside in the Gents. I got up quickly, hoping to restore the situation before the landlord noticed. I grabbed the laughing Mary-Anne, pulled her to one side and unbolted the door. Three potential rugby forwards fell back into the pub. They swore violently, but fortunately were more interested in getting back to their beer than thumping the culprit.

As I breathed a sigh of relief I could see that Mary-Anne still thought her little prank had been a roaring success. She leant against me with an arm round my neck, while she continued to laugh and cry at the same time.

'Mary-Anne, we must go home,' I said firmly as I pushed her from behind and tried to encourage her towards the door. 'You are in one of your giggly moods tonight. Anything might happen.'

'All right then, spoilsport,' she said, with her face fixed in her all too often seen 'naughty little girl expression', and her blue eyes laughing at me as they nearly always did.

Arm in arm we strolled out of the pub into the darkness and across the road, partially lit by street lights, to start walking over the golf course towards the place we called home, St Matthew's Mental Hospital for the Acutely Ill. As we trod on the soft grass of an immaculate fairway, still holding on to each other, I thought how strange it was that a golf course was provided for the supposedly mentally ill, when most of us were so heavily drugged and confused we didn't know who we were, let alone whether to club up or down on the dogleg par four.

As we crossed the golf course, a full moon enabled us to find our way safely round the sand filled bunkers. Mary-Anne had been holding on to me in a very tight and affectionate way when, without warning, as we reached the fine flat grass of a green, she gently broke away and quickly lay down flat on her back on the soft, damp grass. The moon shone light across her body as she lifted her skirt up to her chin and started to giggle.

During the few months that I had known Mary-Anne it appeared, because of her frequent manic moments, that she treated everything in life as a joke, including sex. I looked down at Mary-Anne's body on the grass, which was waiting and quivering for attention. Her smiling face showed very distinctively her well-formed little nose and bright blazened blue eyes which were looking up to the night sky, but I was sure she was laughing at me. Her tongue was flapping between her white teeth in expectation. She looked a mature twenty-two, exciting, full of fun; a temptress designed to dissolve my inhibitions.

Mary-Anne's pale skin, beautiful legs and obvious desire for immediate sex had not passed me by. (Perhaps there was a purpose for a hospital golf course after all, I thought.) Part of me certainly wanted to satisfy Mary-Anne, but I felt physically numb and mentally confused. Had I got loyalties elsewhere, I asked myself? I simply couldn't remember. Was I any damn good at it anyway? I didn't know, but at that moment I had a fear of losing my only friend through incompetence. I cared a lot about Mary-Anne. She was the one person in my extraordinary 'home' surroundings that I felt close to. Her carefree effervescent behaviour helped to soothe my often morbid view of life.

I knelt down beside her and squeezed her soft, white hand. Her smiling face looked attractive and vibrant. I kissed her gently on the cheek. 'Mary-Anne, not on a golf course at ten o'clock at night,' I said pleadingly in her ear. 'Let's go home.'

She sat bolt upright and giggled out the words. 'All right, but you won't escape me for long.'

I felt a tremendous sense of relief that I had not upset her. As I stood up I helped to pull her back to her feet. I allowed a moment for some clothing adjustments and then we walked, clasping hands, towards the lights over the main entrance of this enormous red-brick Victorian building, 'home' to over fifty inmates.

Our building was divided into male and female quarters. Five minutes walk away was the large monstrously ugly building we all feared: the chronic section of

7

St Matthews Hospital – once admitted, it was usually for a life sentence. It was hardly the pride of the city of West Nimbrington in this year of 1965. Very little had changed since the Victorians decided to lock up those people they saw as an embarrassment to society.

Mary-Anne was still giggling as we went through the door. She was definitely in one of her 'high-as-a-kite' frames of mind, which seemed to pursue her for most of the time. However, I found her an attractive tonic, if a rather unpredictable one. She let go of my hand, smiled, staggered a little, giggled again and then started to wend her way down the corridor towards the ladies section. I obediently, and without saying a word, turned the other way and started to walk down the badly-lit, dingy cream-walled passage that led towards my room. On my way I passed a tall man with a slightly greying beard, who always looked as though he had been sleeping rough.

'Hullo Michael, got a gun?' Sam asked, while still walking.

I muttered, 'Sorry, mate,' and carried on.

Sam asked me that same question every day. I could never make out what he would do with a gun if he had one. If he really wanted to kill himself, it was certainly made easy enough in this place. There was no careful check made on the whereabouts of dangerous drugs. Perhaps Sam just collected guns, or maybe he thought I needed one.

I slipped through the door into my small room. It was a very sparse affair – little more than a bed, a door and a window. I turned the light on and lay outstretched on top of my bed. I am classed as a twenty-five-year-old psychotic, but I don't understand why. I know I'm unable to live life in the same apparent 'matter of fact' way that I see most people doing. My whole existence terrifies me. I try to retreat from it, even to the point of wishing to end it all. Mary-Anne is the only small cheerful glimmer of light in my life, and everyone thinks she's crazy – so she may be.

I turned and picked up scraps of papers on which I had scribbled so many poems over the last few months, which helped to give vent to my feelings. Last night's was called 'The Hunt', one of many subjects that I felt strongly about.

> Ere my bit
> With teeth I grit
> As onward trudge my hooves
> A hound, a sound, a horn blasts out!
> Whipped! kicked! now quickly moves
> Froth sweat body towards the rout;
> Tis not my choice to hurry so
> But spurs dig deep, a voice yells 'Go!'
> Wearied, pained, tired of chase,
> I gallop on to keep the pace.
> Astride my back and oh such weight
> Grips leather booted huntsman's fate.
> If I should defy his cruel whip
> Throw him off or feign to trip,
> He would say
> Without delay,
> 'T'is damn stallion stabless beast
> Knackers yard dogs meat to feast!'
> So, each moment I think to defy
> I think to slaughter and don't quite die.

I turned my head to the pillow and sobbed; I lived in a world few people entered or understood.

Just then there was a knock at the door and it promptly opened to reveal a large male nurse, standing in a white coat in front of the pill trolley.

'Collect your pills, Michael,' he said abruptly. 'I haven't got all night.'

I duly did what I was told and was left again, alone in my room, with a handful of coloured pills which I had to take obediently while the nurse was watching me. Some evenings the nurse would give you a mouth check by sticking his short fat fingers inside your cheeks and feeling under your tongue to make sure everything had been swallowed. The pills were very quick-acting; some nights I didn't even get my pyjamas on before I fell asleep.

2

Daylight at St Matthew's usually appears for me when Doris, the cleaner, dressed in her gaudy floral apron, bangs her way through the door and shouts, 'Wake up, Michael,' and drops the *Daily Mirror* on the end of my bed.

I have the same ritual every morning. I get up, grab the newspaper, tear it into four long strips and then tidily piece them together to make a front page, and leave my jigsaw on the floor. Every day, Doris would come in a little later with her broom, sweep up the paper and take it away. I had no idea why I always tore up the newspaper or why I didn't ask for it not to be delivered. With hindsight, Doris, who was to sweep up newspapers off my floor for nine months, deserved a medal for her tactfulness!

What was in store for me this new day at the nick, I wondered, as I pulled on my old brown cord trousers which didn't begin to match the grey striped shirt I had worn every day for the last fortnight. I didn't bother to brush my mop of dark brown hair, as nobody in this place cared what you looked like. After a sort of shave I opened my door and entered that dirty cream corridor once more. I found, sitting on a bench not far from my room, a nun without her head-dress and with short cut hair. She was bent over in her black habit as if she was in some sort of pain. I went and sat next to her. After two minutes silence, I said to her gently, 'What is wrong with you? I haven't met a nun in here before.'

She said, 'Look,' and turned her wrists towards me. There were large scars right across both of them. She continued, saying firmly, 'Don't you ever do this, it makes such a terrible mess.'

10

'Will you come into breakfast with me?' I said, rather taken aback by her attitude to wrist slashing.

'No thank you, I just want to sit here,' she replied.

So as usual I went into the communal dining room on my own, passing 'Have you got a gun, Michael?' on my way.

I looked round, hoping to see Mary-Anne amidst the fifty or so people, but in vain. So I found a seat on a bench by one of the many trestle tables. Either side of me sat people I had never seen before, spooning in prunes with great haste. To accompany the prunes was a selection of slices of hard toast which could easily have been used as floor tiles. The noise in the dining room was quite deafening as some of the more manic patients fought for air space. Fortunately a male nurse grabbed my shoulder and said, 'Michael, Dr Khan wants to see you in his office.'

I liked the idea of leaving the dining room, which I did promptly, but I wasn't so pleased about seeing this pompous doctor, who considered not only that he was God's gift to women, but that all his patients were highly privileged to see him at all.

I went the short distance to Dr Khan's office, and as I crossed the corridor I looked to my left and saw the nun still sitting on her bench. Dr Khan let me sit in a chair facing him over his desk. What a smooth man he was, with his perfectly groomed pitch-black greased hair and light brown skin to match. Yes, I thought, no doubt 'God's gift' to some women but, as far as I knew, of precious little help to his male patients.

'Right, Michael,' he said, looking down at my notes and starting to read aloud, 'I see before you came here you had electro-convulsive therapy twenty-two times. That seems rather a lot. What do you remember of that treatment?'

'Well, I remember being anaesthetized before having up to a hundred volts banged through my head. I suffered loss of memory for a while, and never understood the benefits. I heard that a depressed dog once accidentally had an electric shock and then started to wag its tail, so they now try it on humans!'

'All right, Michael, we are not as crude as that. There is

11

a scientific reason behind the treatment, although it does not seem to have worked for you.'

'I see here,' he said, once more looking down at his notes, 'that on a couple of occasions you have overdosed yourself with pills. Why did you do that?'

What a very stupid question, I thought. There was a silence while I didn't reply. Dr Khan sat upright and said, 'Patients like you make me wonder why I bother. You have been with us for three months and during that time you have shown little progress, so I will try abreaction on you on Friday. Methedrin, the truth drug, used on prisoners of war in order to prise out their innermost secrets, will be injected into your arm. You will become uninhibited, and hopefully tell me all that I need to know about you.

'Today you will go swimming before lunch. Then I want you to prepare a short story for a group therapy meeting. Please write something this time that will have some meaning to the group as a whole,' he continued in his aggressive voice. 'Tomorrow you will relax and stay out of my way.

'Right, you can go now,' he paused as I got out of my chair and started to walk towards the door. Then he yelled, 'For heaven's sake try to walk properly, you're wobbling all over the place.' I was becoming confused by Dr Khan's ever-diminishing amount of understanding help.

As I pulled at the door handle and turned to let myself out, I realized that 'God's gift to women' had not finished.

His eyes caught mine in a long, icy stare, and to my complete surprise he said slowly and firmly, 'By the way, I don't mind you making love to Mary-Anne, as long as you don't do it on top of my desk in front of me!'

'Right,' I mumbled, and left hurriedly, shocked.

Back in the passage I was thinking about Mary-Anne. I must keep her away from Dr Khan. He sounded almost jealous of me for something I had only thought about. He's a lecherous womanizer, and I may not be able to do it on his desk, but he is not having Mary-Anne at all!

As I walked down the passage towards my room, I was still wondering what had made that uncaring creature

12

Khan speak to me like that. It is possible, I thought, that Mary-Anne, in one of many 'high moments', had decided it would be a worthwhile joke to spread the news round the hospital that we were lovers. Perhaps it made her feel more secure in our relationship, or was it to punish me for neglecting her that night on the golf course?

As I reached my room and sat on the end of the bed, I continued to puzzle in my mind. If it was a Mary-Anne joke, then it was a tactless lie of her own creation, but that didn't really worry me. I was much more concerned about Dr Khan's strange reaction. He seemed to be behaving almost like a master at school who might say, 'I know you smoke in the dormitory, Simpson, but don't let me see you, or you're out!' Poor Simpson may have never smoked in his life! The master's bluff was no doubt to shock the truth from his victim, or at the very least a warning shot meant to pierce the innocent mind.

My thoughts were gladly broken as the door moved open, exposing a most unlikely sight. There, standing in the doorway, was a short man in his sixties with balding white hair. He was dressed in a faded khaki Scouts uniform, complete save for the hat. His shorts and pink knobbly knees caught my eyes as I lifted my head and noticed a ruddy, grinning face. The Scout stepped forward and put out his hand. 'How do you do? I'm the hospital Chaplain,' he said politely. 'Call me Joe.'

As I shook Joe's hand it felt to me as though I was clasping something that was warm, limp and only half alive.

'Please come and see me,' he said. 'You will find me in a flower bed. There are lots of flower beds here, and I do all the hoeing.'

It was a nice idea to meet one's religious advisor in a bed of flowers. I was pleased that he seemed so content with his life, and promised that I would look out for him in the garden. As Joe left my room he said, 'Thank you, but I don't hoe on Sundays.'

Dr Khan had said swimming before lunch. I'd better get a move on, it was already midday. I changed into some blue shorts, threw on a dressing-gown and took some hurried steps towards the large indoor pool that was at the back of the building.

The pool was used on most days of the week by at least some of the patients. There was a large shallow end for the many patients who could not swim. However, the deep end was deep enough to entertain a high diving board.

Soon after I had reached the wet tiled edge of the pool and discarded my dressing-gown, I looked round at the ten or so swimmers in the pool, hoping to see Mary-Anne. It wasn't surprising that there was no sign of her, because if I'd stopped to think, I knew perfectly well that men and women were not allowed to use the pool at the same time.

'Michael.' An all-too-familiar voice called out. I looked round, and there walking towards me was Dr Khan, dressed in smooth black swimming trunks and holding up a rugby shirt.

'Michael, I want you to put this on,' he said to my amazement. 'It will help to protect your back,' he added. 'Now I want you to do some rollover dives off the top board. I will tell you what to do.'

I could swim, I knew, but had never tried much diving, so my body hesitated. I was frightened. I adjusted the rugby shirt and then looked at Dr Khan. I could see from his unwavering expression that he meant it. This was not a casual request, it was an order.

Perhaps this is another form of therapy, I thought half-seriously; maybe plunging helplessly from a great height into cold, chlorinated water was good for one's health.

Strangely enough, as it turned out, my diving attempts did help me. I would stand on the top board, be given instructions, and then launch myself into the air, hoping for my body to somersault before hitting the water. I landed on my back many times, was winded on one occasion, but the physical pain I understood and found acceptable. I could not seem to spin enough in order to achieve a graceful, painless hands-first entry. However, I received unusual praise from my instructor.

'Well done, Michael. Get changed now. We will try again another day,' Dr Khan called out in a cheerful voice. I thought, I wish he was in this sort of mood more often, but why did I have to physically hurt myself before he felt able to speak to me kindly?

14

After lunch I set about writing a short story that would definitely have 'some meaning' for the rest of the men in my group therapy class, as demanded by my doctor turned diving instructor.

Once a week, at about 4.00 pm, six of us were encouraged to sit in a circle in the men's common room, in front of a doctor, and talk about our lives or anybody else's lives. The doctor usually had to do a lot of prodding to get anyone to speak at all. However, over the weeks I had learnt that young Paul hated working in his father's conglomerate of high-powered businesses so much that he, when well enough, wanted to retreat to being a librarian. Preferably, I think he meant, in a library that nobody used.

I also had in my group another twenty-five-year-old, Martin, who also felt the answer to contentment in life was to become a librarian. The occasional moment of sanctuary behind a silent column of books did appeal to me, but I would not have made a good librarian. I understood my fellow patients' desire to continue to contribute to life, but in a quiet, gentle and protected way. I was strangely pleased to know Paul and Martin had found something rather than nothing to aim at, but in my particular confused state, life outside this hospital was a blurred, intangible picture.

The alcoholic retired Air Vice-Marshal was my favourite member of our group, although he did not appear to have a name and usually contributed little to our discussions. However, towards the end of his annual six weeks' drying out session he obviously felt better, even virtuous perhaps, at his own achievement. He would talk seemingly for hours about his wife, who got the blame both for him drinking and for him not being allowed to drink. The poor lady didn't seem to be able to do anything right, but if he was able to be honest and serious for a moment, which was unlikely in company, I felt sure he would have admitted he could not live without her.

It was time to join the others in the common room. As I expected, it was Dr Khan who was to lead the group today. I sat down in a comfortable armchair next to Paul, who looked as though he might have been sitting motionless in

15

his chair for several weeks as he gazed with a pale expression at the ceiling at the far end of the room.'

Dr Khan said, 'Right, has anyone written a story?' He must have found it convenient to momentarily forget his instructions to me. His eyes moved slowly round our little circle of disinterested faces. He stopped, as if by chance, when he came to me, and glared at me with those stony cold eyes.

'Yes, I have,' I pleaded.

'Well, get on and read it, I haven't got all day!' he said sharply.

I started gently.

'Two people are treading water in a fast-flowing, deep and dangerous river.' I looked up. No-one in the room except Dr Khan appeared to be listening. I pressed on regardless.

'"What a day it has been," says one. "Disaster has followed disaster. It began when my next door neighbour threw out the baby with the bathwater, and the child has not been seen since. Worse was when her husband, nailing a slate, slid off the roof and broke both his legs. While she was at the hospital, her house burnt down. Hurrying back to see if any of her other children had survived the fire, she was robbed of her handbag in which was all the money she had in the world. On her way to inform the police, she was raped. I tell you, nothing had gone right today. But enough of my worries. Why did you shout help?"'

'Michael, that was more sensible than usual,' said Dr Khan condescendingly. 'Now, anybody, why did that chap shout help?'

To my surprise, Paul, still looking across the room, said, 'Because he can't swim, and nor can I for that matter.'

This remark was followed by a long discussion on who could and couldn't swim. Indeed, the group meeting broke up before the point behind the story was made clear. I thought as I left to get back to my room that it may have been all too obvious to my fellow patients, and so not worth talking about. More likely, few of them had been paying attention. Why didn't Dr Khan lead the discussion? I suppose helping me out was not one of his favourite pastimes. I was annoyed, and vowed that if I was ever

16

asked to write another story for the group it would be meaningless from the beginning, so that no important message could get lost.

3

I remembered it was my day to relax before something I
didn't understand called abreaction took place tomorrow.
I was determined, after so many days of being kept apart
from her, that I would find Mary-Anne, even if I had to
take the whole hospital apart. I ate my breakfast and had
an unusually good shave before setting off in my search. I
knew, of course, that Mary-Anne had a room upstairs in
the ladies' quarters, but it was more than my life was worth
to try that first. If I had been caught in the ladies' area I
might well have been locked in my room and sedated for
twenty-four hours. I decided to try looking for her in the
grounds first.

As I strolled out of the main doors I was reminded by
the sun, the green grass and the flowers that it was a
summer's day. I stood on the concrete steps and looked
about me, but I could see no Mary-Anne. Was she
deliberately hiding from me? Was she up in her room, the
one place I wasn't allowed to go? I put these thoughts
behind me and strode with optimism along the tarmac
path that led to the trees near the edge of the golf course.
A few minutes closer, and I just had a glimpse of the form
of a long, white lady lying under a beech tree. My walk
changed into a jog until I reached the tree. With every
pace I had become more certain that I had at last found
Mary-Anne.

I stood at her feet, breathing heavily, and looked at her
as she lay casually on the grass. She displayed her usual
attractive charm which seemed to be enhanced by her
loose white blouse, yellow cotton skirt and discarded high-
heeled shoes. I felt like trying them on. I wanted to touch

18

everything that was hers.

I looked towards her eyes and pleaded with her.

'Where have you been? I've missed you so much.'

She turned her curly blond head and looked up at me. Her childish smile and piercing blue eyes hadn't changed since our last meeting, nor had her ability to laugh at me.

'Where do you think I've been?' she retorted. 'In the same damn place as you, of course!'

'Mary-Anne, do you have the same doctor as me?'

'How do I know?' she said unhelpfully.

'Well,' I said, 'is your doctor Dr Khan?'

'No, I have a lady doctor, Dr Janet Spicer, she's very nice to me.'

'Well,' I persisted, 'do you know Dr Khan? Have you ever spoken to him?'

'I've seen him around,' she said. 'Why do you ask?'

I realized my line of enquiry was futile and that Mary-Anne was not likely to admit that she had told my doctor that we were lovers or knew that his desk was out of bounds! Anyway, who cares, I was wasting valuable time.

I sat down on the soft grass next to Mary-Anne. I picked up her left hand and started to play with her fingers. I was thinking what beautiful soft skin she had to go with her pianist fingers when she started to giggle as she lay on the ground. She said, 'Michael, you can borrow that hand if you like, but what shall I do with the rest of me?'

I put the hand down and tried to stop being pathetic. I leant backwards and gave her a quick kiss on the lips, which immediately made her start giggling. I found her giggling most atractive because it suited me to think it meant she was happy. I just hoped that it was not all at my expense, and that she took our friendship as seriously as I did. How was I to find out what she really thought? I looked at the writing on the notebook which lay in the grass beside her. She saw my gaze, picked up her book and said, 'Would you like to hear it?'

'Yes,' I said, 'please.'

Her soft voice spoke some incoherent words: 'The earth, the turf, for what it's worth, lies topsyturvy over curving limes.'

'Is that all?' I said.

19

'Yes. Don't you think it's good?'

The mind of this young lady seemed to confuse me even more, and I had to wonder where these topsyturvy limes had come from. Poetry should know no bounds within the limits of a person's imagination, but Mary-Anne's writing wasn't saying anything to me except perhaps 'while we lie here for better times'.

Why was I so drawn to Mary-Anne in her ever-merry world? I puzzled to myself. The more she laughed at me, the more I loved and needed her. I envied her casual, gay, abandoned approach to life. She gave to me an insight into a type and shade of existence that I was unable to find for myself. Yes, I thought, I do know why.

I looked at Mary-Anne's soft white face being lit up by the sunlight and knew how exciting it was to be with her, even if she never seemed to want to step inside the emotional caring arms that I kept holding out for her and us.

I had to feel my body pressed against her. Now was the time. I lay almost on top of Mary-Anne and ran the fingers of both my hands through her blond hair. Then, with my 'love' in a totally relaxed state, I held her head firmly, kissed gently at first then pressed my lips against her mouth. She was the most beautiful being I had ever known.

I pushed myself up slightly so that I could look into those clear blue eyes, and hoped to read a reaction in her expression. Her eyes were smiling into mine, followed by her gentle giggle.

'Do you love me, Mary-Anne?' I asked in a whisper.

With a glowing grin and her so very blue eyes fixed on mine, she started to sit up. I let her. Then, in an uncontrollable state of helpless caring emotion, I threw my arms round her, buried my head in her chest and cried violently. I was like a small boy desperately clinging to his mother. I needed her warmth and her confidence. Tears rolled down my face and I shook hysterically. Mary-Anne held me with an arm pulling me to her and a hand stroking my head, as though she consoled grown men in tears every day of her life.

Gradually, with the comfort of the girl I loved, I became

calm, let go my grip on her, sat up and gazed through blurred, bewildered eyes at Mary-Anne. 'I'm sorry,' I whimpered, as if in disgrace.

'Don't be sorry,' she said, smiling gently. 'I cry sometimes, too.'

'Do you really?' I replied, as though I didn't believe it possible of my 'laughing girl'.

Our sunny spot under the beech tree was far from idyllic; every few moments someone would walk past and give us a good stare. One outgoing young man with hair down to his waist stopped and looked at us for a moment. He was new at the hospital and was known as Jamie. He had apparently been a pop singer until he got involved in the drug scene in London and was eventually sent to us. He seemed a nice young man, although his behaviour was very odd. Just as he was leaving us he did a forward roll in the ground, then stood up and announced delightedly that he was an egg! He didn't wait for a reply, but used some strange dance step to propel himself back towards the hospital. I was to learn later that Jamie was a clever young man who had worked out an unlikely 'Master Plan' for an early discharge from this hospital.

My eyes and face had dried a little after the distraction created by Jamie. Knowing that at St Matthews my tears needed no explanation, I cleared my throat and asked Mary-Anne enthusiastically, 'Will you come into town with me this afternoon, please?'

'All right,' she said, with a cheerful grin on her face. 'I will meet you after lunch under this tree.'

We both stood up and Mary-Anne brushed some grass cuttings off her clothes with a brisk flick of her wrist. She slid her feet into her shoes and picked up her notebook with one hand while offering me the other. I clasped it tightly and held it as we walked in silence back to the main doors, where we parted to go to our segregated areas.

I didn't consider what I was eating for lunch, I was too excited thinking of how I was going to spend the afternoon with Mary-Anne. She had been quite wonderful this morning, 'my gentle angel'. Indeed, as I continued to reflect, she had seemed happy without being wildly giggly to the point where she would not take anything seriously, least of all me. I had always thought that she was lucky to have manic moods that varied in intensity and made her appear dramatically happy, particularly as I was so different to her and was swept into tears with seemingly little or no provocation many times a day. I felt we must be good for each other. However, I did realize that, when Mary-Anne's mania was at its peak, she became so uninhibited and carefree that at such times she put herself at very considerable risk in the world outside our protected 'home'. I thought of a few of the endless possible ways she might behave. She might book a large concert hall for a personal performance on the triangle, or order a Rolls-Royce she didn't need and couldn't begin to pay for, or quite possibly stand on a table at 'The George' and dance round naked for the pleasure of the customers. Anything could happen. I vowed I would always try to look after Mary-Anne when she was 'high', but regretted terribly that I was not with her all of the time.

To be allowed out of the grounds, we both had to get our appropriate senior staff nurse's permission. Graham was mine, a likeable chap, if coldly efficient. He was only about twenty-eight, with dark brown hair cut very short, for reasons of hygiene perhaps.

I spotted Graham in the corridor organizing the pill trolley. As he saw me approach he said, 'Hullo Michael, how are you?'

What a remarkably stupid question, I thought. 'I don't know,' I said, 'but if I go out to Nimbrington this afternoon I'm sure it will help.'

'Well,' said Graham, pausing for thought before saying, 'on your own?'

'No, with a friend,' I replied, slightly annoyed.

'Might that friend be Mary-Anne Cheyney?' he said, with the smile of a man who was about to win first prize in a quiz programme for two-year-olds.

'Yes.'

'You see a lot of . . .'

I interrupted Graham and said with some force, 'Can I go or not?'

'Yes, OK,' he said in a condescending way and looked down at his pill pots, clearly tired of my unstimulating company. I needed nothing more from Graham, and in my haste to get to my room I forgot to thank him. I grabbed my cheque book and a few pounds from my bedside locker. Then I quickly pushed myself out of my door and started to make my way to the beech tree.

There was no Mary-Anne at the beech tree – or was there? Yes, I could hear a slightly stifled laugh from behind the tree trunk. I ran round and grabbed my playful girl.

'I was going to make you wait much longer, but as usual I couldn't help giving the game away,' she said with a broad smile on her face, which exposed a set of perfect white teeth. I pulled her towards me. We were very conveniently the same height, which meant we met at eye level when standing together. I loved looking closely at her face, but I was slightly concerned as there seemed to be the twinkling expression of a would-be prankster about her this afternoon.

We chose to set off by way of the tarmac path leading towards the main gates which gave a direct approach to the town centre. Mary-Anne looked happy as she swung her arms in the air, and nearly let go of her handbag. 'Isn't it the most wonderful day?' she said to the blue sky, while skipping a little and then glancing at me.

Either side of the main gates were large flowerbeds. Both of us couldn't fail to notice a small, rotund figure dressed as a Scout, wielding a hoe in the middle of one bed. We stopped, and I called out, 'Hey, Joe! It's Michael, remember me?'

Joe turned and smiled in a well-meaning but silly sort of way. 'There are too many roses in this flowerbed. There is not enough room for me,' he said crossly, while hitting the odd rose with his hoe for good measure. I felt a tug on my arm, so we said goodbye to our gardening friend and walked on.

I said to Mary-Anne, 'Wouldn't it be terribly sad if over-crowded plants or anything else put Joe out of a job?'

She looked at me and said hurriedly, 'I want to go to the shoe shop, the dress shop, yes, all the shops.'

Outside the gates I felt nervous of the traffic speeding past, the noise and the confidence of the pedestrians' faces as they walked with the apparent knowledge of where they were going. At times like this I desperately needed Mary-Anne with her daring boldness, which never ceased to amaze me.

As we stood on the edge of the pavement facing some of West Nimbrington's shops, I remembered that we were not a good combination at crossing the road. Mary-Anne tended to walk across without concerning herself about such details as avoiding fast-moving cars, whereas I used to look, look again, then wait and dither. On this occasion we held hands. I did the looking while Mary-Anne pulled me. However, she let go of me in the middle of the road, preferring to run the rest of the way. She turned her head back to me and shouted excitedly, 'I'll meet you at the dress shop.'

I, too, started to run, not wanting to lose sight of her, for both our sakes.

In the dress shop, where I felt particularly out of place, there was an enormous display of skirts and dresses. A very good selection, I thought.

Mary-Anne announced with a coarse laugh, 'Most of this stock is older than I am!' Then she turned to the far from amused lady assistant and said, still chuckling, 'Have you got a really ravishing full-length red silk ballgown for a special occasion?'

Looking astonished, but holding her composure, the assistant said, 'No, sorry, Madam.'

I gripped Mary-Anne's arm and led her hurriedly out of the shop. 'What special occasion?' I asked.

'I might have worn it to breakfast tomorrow,' she laughed.

'To celebrate us having porridge, not prunes?' I suggested sarcastically.

'No, come on, Michael,' she said imploringly, 'let's just enjoy ourselves. I want to make you happy, very happy,' and added with a smile, 'if you will let me.'

The next shop that caught her eye was a toy shop. Sitting in the window was a big, cuddly pink elephant with long ears, a curled trunk and large enchanting eyes. I had to think fast. I had to stop Mary-Anne going in there, or she might have tried to buy a lorry-load of soft toys. I said quickly, 'Kate's Café is in the next street somewhere; why don't we go and look for it?'

'OK,' she said happily, and firmly squeezed my hand.

Kate's Café was clean and bright. It had several round oak-stained tables with small oval back chairs set round them. The waitress showed us to a table and gave us both a menu card.

'I'm going to have a coconut cream cake, a glass of Coke and a can to take away,' announced Mary-Anne very firmly.

'I would like chocolate cake and a glass of Coke, please,' I said more softly.

The waitress hardly needed her pad before she set off to collect our order. Leaning forward towards me, Mary-Anne made a comment on my choice. 'I never eat chocolate, it brings me out in spots.'

'What does coconut do to you?' I said, being flippant.

'Wait and see,' she said with a big grin.

The café was deserted, except for two elderly ladies drinking tea in the far corner. If they had known where we had come from, they might well have said, 'I don't think they should allow St Matthews' patients to wander round the town. You don't know what they might do next.'

My paranoid mind was brought back to reality as the waitress returned with our food. She placed the Coke on the table and put a plate of cake in front of both of us. Mary-Anne immediately picked up hers with her fingers and started eating it with great gusto.

'This is delicious,' she said with her mouth full. 'Why don't you start yours?'

I tried to stop myself from smiling as I said, 'I seem to have got the wrong order.'

'What's wrong with it?' she said, still munching.

'It's coconut!' I exclaimed.

'Oh no!' she said, grinning. 'I've nearly eaten a whole piece of chocolate cake. Why didn't you stop me?'

'I was too late,' I said with a smile. She laughed loudly. Even the old ladies turned and looked at her.

I had nothing to eat because of the waitress's minor mistake, but it did give me the chance to watch Mary-Anne getting covered in cream. She didn't mind how much of a mess she was making. She was enjoying herself.

While watching Mary-Anne eat, I decided to push my feet under the table until I was touching her. In spite of our quaint surroundings I felt a desperate need to tell her that I loved her and that she would always be the most beautiful girl in the world to me. I needed her so much. My past was a haze in my memory. My future was totally uncertain. I survived from day to day with little to live for or love, except for this exceptional young lady who completely mesmerised me. I looked straight into her eyes and said gently, 'Mary-Anne, promise you won't ever leave me?'

She replied, still licking cream off her long white fingers, 'Why should I want to?' She moved on quickly to another subject. 'Michael, let's do something really exciting,' she said, giggling. I was reminded that she was not one to dwell on what I considered serious matters. 'Let's go for a drive,' she suggested eagerly after a little thought.

'Mary-Anne, you can't drive and I can't remember when I last drove, and anyway, we haven't got a car.'

'Is that a problem?' she said, now laughing uncontrollably. There was something infectious about her moods of extreme happiness.

'All right,' I said, 'there is a garage down the road; let's see if they can lend us a car.'

It took a few moments to pay our bill. Then I looked round, and to my surprise could not see Mary-Anne. Perhaps she is waiting outside, I thought. I ran out to the pavement.

'Oh my God!' I cried. She was walking down the middle of the road, drinking a can of Coke. There were cars racing past her in both directions. Quite out of character I ran into the road, hardly looking, and grabbed her. She was giggling and Coke was running down her chin.

'You'll get killed!' I screamed.

'No I won't,' she spluttered. 'I know where I'm going to, the garage.'

'The morgue, more likely,' I said, dragging her to the safety of the pavement, at which point she cried with excitement and ran the hundred yards to the small garage, with me chasing behind her. I was now certain that the car was not a good idea, but was unable to upset her recklessly happy and determined mood. I would just have to protect her somehow. There was a large shiny new blue car on the forecourt.

'This will do,' said Mary-Anne, trying one of the doors.

'This is for sale,' I insisted. 'We just want to borrow one.'

At last a bearded man strode out towards us.

'Are you interested in our new model, Madam?' he politely enquired of Mary-Anne.

'No, she isn't,' I interrupted loudly and desperately. 'We would just like to hire a little car for a few hours.'

'Come this way, Sir,' said the bearded man, pointing to a battered door with 'office' written on it. I held Mary-Anne very firmly by the hand and followed the gentleman.

After fifteen minutes of dealing with confusing bits of paper and, against my better wishes, paying for the minimum hire period of twenty-four hours, we had our car. It was an old red Mini, rusting at the seams. I sat behind the wheel, with Mary-Anne sitting beside me. I felt terrified and discovered I had acquired a slight tremor in my hands. Mary-Anne was excited and noisily kept fidgeting. Could I remember how to drive a car, I wondered? I had a licence in my wallet, so I must have known how to at one time. I remembered it was like the cheque book I had used earlier. I had it in my pocket, but did I have any money in a bank?

For Mary-Anne's sake I turned the ignition key and prayed. I managed to get us onto the road and to turn left, which saved the possible difficulty of crossing the road.

'Why are we going so slowly?' she said.

'I'm in the wrong gear,' I replied helplessly. I did not dare to take my eyes off the road even for a moment, so I found myself feeling blindly for the gear lever with my left hand. My hand kept coming to rest on Mary-Anne's right knee.

'You like my knee a lot,' she said, pulling her skirt off it.

'I am simply trying to find the gear lever,' I insisted. 'What have you done with it?'

'Well, I haven't given it to anybody,' she said, chuckling to herself.

'Well, please move your legs over,' I pleaded. 'No, not towards me, the other way. Got it at last,' I muttered as I moved us up to third.

The strain of driving the car with my level of anxiety and complete lack of confidence was making me feel quite unwell and a little dizzy.

'Why does everyone keep overtaking us?' Mary-Anne said observantly. Without waiting for a reply, she went on, 'Let's go to Eaton Square and see Daddy's flat.'

'You must be crazy,' I said, continuing to look at the road in front of me. 'I could no more drive this car all the way to London than fly. In fact, I will have gone far enough when we get to the gap in those fir trees on the right just ahead of us,' I said emphatically.

I pulled over and switched off the ignition. I let go of the steering wheel with a feeling of great relief, tilted my head back over the top of the seat and breathed heavily.

'We haven't come very far,' Mary-Anne commented. 'We could have walked as far as this!' She then laughed infectiously. I turned and managed to smile at her.

'You need a better chauffeur, Madam,' I said, meaning it.

'Don't be silly,' she said kindly. 'I like the one I've got,' and then she leaned over the handbrake and put her arm round my shoulders. Although it seemed inevitable, I was upset to see Mary-Anne undoing the buttons on the front of her white blouse with her free hand. Was she, I thought, honestly thinking that we should try to make love in the front of this cramped tin box? Even if you were willing and able, you would need to be a contortionist. In any case, I was far from willing. I knew her body was beautiful and one day, if I was ever well enough, I'm sure I would want to satisfy both of us.

With all the buttons undone now, there was a giggle before reaching for the bra clip. 'I said I would get you one day,' she laughed confidently.

'The car is too small,' I said hopefully. I daren't tell Mary-Anne in case she rejected me as a close friend because of it, so I kept my thoughts to myself as I reflected that ever since I had been at St Matthews I had felt impotent and pathetic. It didn't normally worry me, but in this situation I felt like an invalid.

Seeing Mary-Anne stripped to the waist made me weep at my helplessness. 'You are beautiful,' I said gently, and then, with tears in my eyes, I bowed my head and pressed the side of my face against her warm breasts. 'My darling, please forgive me,' I cried at the sound of my desperate appeal to her understanding.

'Michael, I'm very patient with special people,' she said with a grin. I felt enormously thankful, but how many special people were there, I wondered as I sat back up in my seat? Perhaps it was just a turn of phrase, I thought, to make myself feel better.

Mary-Anne gave me a firm kiss on top of my nose, and then quickly dressed herself.

'Let's go!' she said, no doubt trying to dismiss from her mind what might have happened. She banged her head on the dashboard, putting the headlights on and off, and cried, 'Hi Ho, Silver!' We drove back to the garage as if I had not just faced one of the biggest emotional traumas of my life. I drove a little better this time because we were now going back to the garage, and not away to 'no-man's land'.

We dumped the car on the forecourt as we were unable to find our bearded friend or anyone else.

I looked at my watch and muttered, 'Half past seven.' It was later than we thought, but neither of us cared. It had been a wonderful day. Mary-Anne was so full of life, and in her own way I believed she really did care about me and my feelings.

We walked quietly hand in hand up to St Matthews' front door. Then we separated with a kiss and a smile, back to our own rooms, both of us pleased to know a little more about each other.

That evening, before going to sleep I lay on top of my bed and thought about Mary-Anne. She had an amazing visible strength of personality, and nothing seemed to frighten her. I found her strength immensely attractive and complimentary to my constant desire to withdraw from life. Indeed, I would never have dreamt that today I would hire a car and drive it. That was a most unexpected achievement, but it happened entirely because of the determination and persuasion of Mary-Anne.

In spite of her tough, jovial exterior, I knew now she was also a kind and loving person. She not only had put up with my tears but had accepted my lack of desire for sex. Sometimes she was my 'mother', an older, sensible, caring woman who hugged me when I cried. At other times she was my dearest and closest friend; the contemporary companion that I never wanted to lose. She had become part of my very being. I could not bear to imagine my confused world without her. The very thought made me feel helpless, desolate and unable to go on. I blanked off such a possibility in my mind, unable to think about it. I quickly reflected back to that ever-cheerful smiling lady who would be safely tucked up in her bed by now in the same building as me. That was a comforting thought.

Graham pushed open the door and exposed the pill trolley. 'You look half-asleep already, Michael,' he said observantly. 'Did you overdo it in the town today? Some of our ladies can be a bit of a handful.'

As I got up off the bed to collect my small plastic pill pot I was thinking aggressively, if Graham says one unkind word about Mary-Anne I will punch him on the nose, or anywhere else for that matter. Fortunately for both of us, I just mumbled, 'I had a good day.'

After swallowing my pills I then put up with the distasteful indignity of a mouth check, and did so without biting his fingers.

As he left, I thought if Graham does not trust me to swallow my pills, then he is unlikely to believe anything I say to him. Perhaps he thought I was going to store my pills ready for a grand exit, or perhaps give them to another patient, sending them to sleep in the middle of the day in order to avoid some type of therapy. His excuse for feeling around inside my mouth would be, 'It's just one of those things that a staff nurse is trained to do.' No discretion was allowed. If he was told to shave his head, he would certainly do it. He had got very close to it already.

I sat on the edge of my bed and thought more realistically for a moment. Graham was helping to look after about fifty patients with very differing needs, most thought to be unpredictable and rather confused. He needed every bit of his training to survive his job and to stop the whole place turning into chaos. However, he was unaware that if ever he dared to make an unfavourable remark about my lady, Mary-Anne, I would explode with rage in my attempts to defend her. He had got pretty close this evening.

The pills were having an effect on me. My eyes were nearly shut as I flopped my limp body into a sleeping position. I fell asleep holding tightly on to my pillow and thinking briefly of the only person who really mattered in my life.

4

1.

Unexpected by me, the best day of my life was about to begin. I started to get dressed when the door to my room was flung open by Doris and her curly dyed red hair, who dropped my newspaper on to the end of my bed and left abruptly. Without hesitating, I tore up the paper and pieced it together on the floor. Perhaps I thought other people tore up their newspapers before they had even read them, a fact that might help to justify my strange ritual.

Unusually, I had another visitor before breakfast. This time it was a tall, young, bespectacled staff nurse that I had never seen before. He had a very thin face with a hooked, bent nose that looked to me not unlike a tin-opener. He spoke to me very briskly. 'Michael Simpson, no breakfast for you. Abreaction at nine o'clock. I will fetch you.'

I sat on my bed and pondered my fate. Dr Khan had said I was going to be given a truth drug. Did this mean he could ask me questions about Mary-Anne and I would be helpless not to answer honestly? My relationship with Mary-Anne was private to all save each other, and particularly private to that inquisitive doctor of mine.

Dr Khan might say to his drugged patient, 'Do you love Mary-Anne?'

My honest reply would have to be, 'Yes, passionately. I want to be with her forever.'

I can hear him saying with a lecherous smile, 'Have you slept with her?'

'No,' would be my reply, but he would not believe me, and this would throw doubts on the supposed infallibility of his drug.

It was fear and misgivings that I felt as the staff nurse led me firmly by the arm to the small square room known as 'the cell', at the very end of the corridor. I knew there was a tubular metal bed and a small wooden chair in there. The door of this grim, apparently windowless room was shut hard and loudly behind us. Dr Khan had been waiting for me. He was wearing a white coat, and his shiny light brown fingers were playing eagerly with a syringe. He seemed to be smiling in anticipation of the pleasure this treatment was going to give him.

'Right, lie on the bed, Michael, and pull up your shirt sleeve,' Dr Khan said, looking a little more serious. 'I am going to give you an injection of Methedrin,' he said as I obediently positioned myself with my back on the bed and rolled up my right shirt sleeve. He continued in his matter-of-fact way: 'Then I will ask you questions, and staff nurse Rambling,' referring to the unfortunate-looking young man sitting in the chair with pen and pad poised to record some gems of knowledge from my subconscious, 'will make notes.' Then he stated with complete confidence, 'You will not remember what you have said when you leave this room in about one hour's time.'

I felt alarmed, and pleaded with my would-be assailant, 'Why are you doing this to me?'

'I thought I had already told you,' retorted the doctor, who appeared today to be still more foreign than usual. He then went on to reluctantly explain. 'I am going to try to revive your forgotten or repressed ideas of the event that may have first caused you to be unwell.'

I didn't entirely believe him. I had only just been told that I would remember nothing of the interview. A particularly worrying thought crossed my mind. Was I going to be an 'open book' to a man who already didn't appear to like me, so that indeed he would know more about me than I knew about myself? He might then be able to manipulate my whole life more than he did already, and with frightening confidence.

Dr Khan had run out of the limited time that he allowed for himself to talk to me before the injection. He stood

33

beside the bed, stooping slightly, while his shiny light brown hands hovered over me with a firm grip on a full syringe.

'I want to find a nice, prominent vein,' he muttered to himself as he looked at the middle of my upturned arm.

I sat up. Dr Khan was not even in the room. Staff nurse Rambling looked sternly at me through his metal-framed glasses as he still sat almost motionless in his chair. Why worry? Why worry about anything, I thought? I had a fizzing sensation in my head and an exciting, light as a feather tingling feeling in my body. I slid off the bed and announced, 'I'm going.'

I slipped excitedly out of the cell door. The staff nurse just stared as I went, and did not try to stop me. In the corridor I jumped in the air and waved my arms above my head. I was so happy. I felt a different person, I felt elated, sky-high! I danced and sang – although there were other people in the corridor I did not mind. I had no inhibitions at all. I could do anything. I was so delighted to be alive. I saw a young female nurse some yards in front of me. I ran up to her, grabbed her, swung her round, laughing as I did it. She cried out, 'Let me go!' and ran down the corridor to get away from me. Life was really the most tremendous fun. There were no rules in my life. There was no longer any feeling of shyness, conscience or guilt in my world.

I saw young Jamie coming towards me, his waist-length fair hair seemed to have grown. I rolled on the ground in front of him, trying to mimic his egg. He laughed at me and put one arm behind his back to form a handle and the other drooping out in front of him to form a spout, and declared he was a teapot! I smiled and gave him a friendly slap on the back before rushing down the corridor towards the ladies' quarters.

I must get to Mary-Anne's room, I thought. Right now, I could be the strong one. I could do anything with her or for her, nothing was a problem.

I ran up the stairs that led to Mary-Anne's room. When I arrived at her door it was to find it was wide open, which gave me a back view of a man dressed in a black cassock and wearing a clerical collar. This must be the real hospital chaplain. From where I was standing I could only just see the curly blonde top of Mary-Anne's head as she lay on her bed, obviously listening intently to this gentleman. Even in my uninhibited state I felt this was not the moment to see her, and decided I would catch up with her later.

At the bottom of the stairs, still feeling highly elated and like somebody who only knew happiness, I met a lady staff nurse. She took one look at me and was about to say, 'You are not allowed in this part of the hospital, what do you think you are doing?' but before she could speak I had thrown my arms round her ample body and was giving her a long, firm hug while I laughed uncontrollably. Not content with hugging her, I decided she might look better with no clothes on. I pushed her back a little and then started to unbutton her uniform. She screamed, escaped from me and ran awkwardly down to the men's area to get help and report me.

I laughed and joked with everybody I met, putting my arms round some people, kissing others. My light-hearted actions were quite out of my control. I was really enjoying myself. A moment later, two well-built male nurses dressed in their white cotton jackets came running up the corridor and grabbed me. With one strong man holding on to either side of me, I had no chance to resist being led back to my room and left to sit on my bed. My door was slammed shut by the nurses. A moment later, to my considerable surprise, a very attractive female nurse came into my room. She sat on the end of my bed with her back to me, saying, 'I've been sent to keep an eye on you.'

All I could see of the nurse was a single blond plait running down her back. It was too tempting. I leant forward, gripped the plait and, as it reminded me of a bell cord, I tugged it twice, as though I was ringing for service, and called out, 'Let's have another bottle of port!'

In my continued excitement I didn't let go of the plait, but started to undo it. I took the elastic off the end, but by this time the young nurse, who clearly had shown through her patience that she understood the effects on me of my recent treatment, and who had tried to show sympathy rather than fear by staying in my room, got up and said to me, 'You need a male nurse, I will get one.'

She disappeared out of the door for only a few seconds before the quiet, unfortunate-looking nurse Rambling arrived and stood by the door, staring at me.

He said, 'If you calm down a little by this evening, as I anticipate, you will be allowed to go to the common room.'

For several hours I lay on my bed, then paced round the room, glancing occasionally out of the window. All I could really think of was that somehow today must go on for ever. I must find Mary-Anne alone and let her know, realize and appreciate what tremendous fun I am, and how I can make her happy, ecstatically happy, I thought, happier than anyone had ever made her or ever would. While I was pacing up and down I was being closely observed by the staff nurse's stern eyes as he leant back against the corner of the door. I knew I couldn't get out of this room to Mary-Anne until this evening, and then only if I had calmed down. Calmed down, he had said. How did he expect me to calm down? I was over the moon. I was like an excited greyhound held in his trap at the start of a race. I started to plead with the nurse to let me go, but he didn't even bother to answer. If I had just knocked the staff nurse out of the way and got back into the corridor to look for Mary-Anne they would certainly have sent me across to a padded cell to cool down. So I sat on the edge of the bed, my body still tingling, my head still swimming as though I'd had several bottles of Scotch, and tried to resign myself to my predicament, although I still felt especially good, as I had never felt before.

I smiled and giggled to myself as my head bent forward and I looked at the floor. I thought, oh yes, of course, this staff nurse in my room must know all my secret thoughts.

'Staff nurse,' I said, looking up and smiling broadly, 'staff nurse, what did you find out about me this morning?'

Rambling looked at me without exchanging my smile, and said almost in a monotone, 'If we had learnt anything, I certainly wouldn't be in a position to tell you. But in actual fact we learnt nothing at all.'

I don't know why I bothered to ask him, I thought to myself, chuckling at his reply and turning my eyes to the floor, because I simply didn't believe him. If, as they said, this treatment had been used on prisoners of war in order to obtain vital secrets and it had worked, then surely they must have got something from my subconscious. Perhaps I was just empty-headed, I laughed to myself. I looked up at Rambling and said, 'Did Dr Khan ask me about my friends, and what did I say?'

'I am not at liberty to discuss this any further. I have already told you we learnt nothing that mattered.'

At last Rambling and I had both tired of each other's company, and so, in a relatively calm frame of mind, I was taken to the common room. I was left to sit quietly with the distant company of several people sitting in comfortable armchairs, gently talking. I noticed Paul and Sam were talking together, and I was not far from them as I sat next to Jamie. I had calmed down quite a bit since my injection that morning, but I still had this fizzing sensation inside my head which made me prefer to laugh rather than smile. Jamie turned his mountainous locks to talk to me. I wondered what he was going to change into next. However, he surprised me by asking, 'Are you going to church tomorrow?'

'No, I'm not, Jamie,' I said, a little surprised by his question, as I had not been to church for several years. 'Why are you going?' I asked out of curiosity.

'Well, I am hoping to be Christened in a few weeks. In two weeks, actually,' he said, and meant it.

'That's a nice idea,' I said, 'but you don't strike me as the sort of chap who'd be religious.'

'Well, I am,' he said firmly. 'At least as long as I am kept in this place.'

'What do you mean?' I said.

'Well,' he explained. 'If all goes according to plan, I will be confirmed in a month's time, then . . .'

'Then,' I interrupted, 'then you will train for the priesthood, I suppose.'

'No!' he said. 'Don't be ridiculous. You see, once the staff and my doctor see that I am a changed person with deep religious beliefs, then they will consider me cured, let me go, and I can go back to my music.'

'And drugs, Jamie?' I mentioned carefully.

'No, I won't touch them again, even though it's not one of the Ten Commandments,' he said, with a not very reassuring grin.

'No more eggs or teapots, Jamie?' I asked with a smile.

'I've got to stop doing that,' he said, wondering how he would manage it. 'It makes the staff worry about me, and that's bad.'

On reflecting, I said to Jamie, 'I think your plan will work. I wish you luck with it.'

'I knew I needed to ask Jamie a favour; I also knew he would willingly carry it out for me. I had learnt from my first day in this strange backwater home of ours that we were a very closely knit community. There was a tremendous sense of understanding and caring between the patients, even though there was a wide age range and varied differences of illness. We all suffered in our various ways and had difficulties in coping with normal life. As I turned to Jamie, with his young face partially obscured by his very long hair, I knew with complete confidence that he would help me.

'Jamie, I must go and see Mary-Anne.'

'She'll be in the ladies' quarters,' he said, with some alarm.

'I know that,' I said, wondering why he stated the obvious. 'But it's worse than that,' I said anxiously. 'I've had some sort of treatment today and the staff nurse doesn't want me to move from this chair until I go back to my room tonight. Can you think up some excuse if they come in here and check up on me? I won't be long. Tell them I'm in the loo, will you, or something like that.'

'Sure, fine,' said Jamie, quite pleased to feel that he'd got something to do.

'Okay, mate,' I said, 'I'm off.'

I walked with an air of confidence back into the corridor and started to head towards the ladies' section. There seemed to be no nurses about. As I neared the ladies' common room, which was the first door I came to in the area, I heard the most incredible singing, and stopped in my tracks and listened. The most beautiful soprano voice I had ever heard was singing the beautiful allegro 'One Fine Day' from *Madam Butterfly*. I couldn't believe that anybody in this hospital could sing so exquisitely well, and, what is more, I knew that voice better than my own. It was my darling Mary-Anne's. I took a few quiet paces and then pushed the door to the ladies' common room open slightly. Mary-Anne was playing, as she sang, a small grand piano up at the far end of the room.

The female patients were dressed in an extraordinary range of clothes. In that room there must have been somebody prepared for almost any function you could think of. There was one overweight lady with a kind face who was simply dressed in a tee-shirt and trousers, whereas there were some in skirts and some in smart dresses. I slid quietly into the room and stood behind one of the big armchairs and looked towards Mary-Anne. I could only see her head and shoulders above the piano. I could see her facial expression varying with the change of intensity of the music. Her singing, like herself, was very strong and forceful. When she had finished, everybody, including myself, clapped loudly. She stood up and, to my amazement, was wearing a beautiful black ballgown with small, neatly-made shoulder straps. I reflected that perhaps when we were in the dress shop together she did, after all, have a very real purpose for the dress she had tried to order.

Mary-Anne never ceased to amaze me. I wished I had a camera and a tape recorder so that I could always listen to Mary-Anne's voice and always see the picture of her as she was this evening, looking particularly lovely with her blond hair contrasting beautifully with her black gown. Although I was at the opposite end to Mary-Anne, she caught my eye and called out, 'Michael, what are you doing here?'

All the women in the room promptly turned their heads towards me and then roared with laughter at the thought of a man being in their common room. I walked boldly through the armchairs towards Mary-Anne and then, reaching her in front of the piano, partly for my sake but also for the sake of the cheerful smiling eyes in my audience, delighted by my intrusion, I put my arms round Mary-Anne's bare shoulders and kissed her on the cheek. There was a roar of delight from the onlookers.

Without warning, Mary-Anne grabbed me and pushed me below the height of the piano and held one hand on the back of my mop head of dark brown hair to indicate to me, 'Don't stand up.' A male staff nurse had just looked round the corner of the door.

He called out, 'Has anyone seen Michael Simpson?'

There was a slight giggle which I thought would have given the game away to the nurse, but then a loud, unanimous reply of, 'No, we haven't.'

I realised that Jamie's excuses for me had run out of time. The nurse went away to continue his search. I stood up, told Mary-Anne her singing was quite wonderful, and then made my way back between the chairs, kissing two or three ladies on request. It made me feel pleased as I left the ladies that they had wanted me to kiss them.

I scuttled down the corridor straight into my room, shut the door and laid on the bed, trying to make myself look as if I had been part of the furniture for the last hour. Soon there was a knock on the door and, before a reply, in came a tired-looking staff nurse Rambling. He was rather short of breath and said in desperation, 'Where have you been, for heaven's sake, Michael?'

'I was in the loo,' I said, trying to look casual.

'Then why did Jamie say you were in the chapel?' retorted the nurse angrily.

'Jamie is a very religious chap, nurse, and he would like to think that I had gone to chapel.'

'Well, at least you're back here now. It has been rather an unusual day for you, but don't think of going anywhere else because I shall be standing outside your door until Graham comes with the medications.'

Left alone in my room once more it suddenly occurred to me Dr Khan was right. I did not remember what I had said to him this morning! Would I ever know what he had learnt about me, I wondered? Graham appeared with the trolley.

2.

The next day I woke up feeling limp, lethargic and as

40

though I lived at the bottom of a dark, damp bucket. I knew now what people meant by drug withdrawal symptoms. If Dr Khan had come through the door and offered me another jab of Methedrin, I know I would have keenly accepted.

I moped about the room, trying slowly to get dressed. As I sat on my bed, knowing I was missing breakfast, I knew that now I was only too aware of how easy it must have been for young Jamie to get hooked to the London drugs scene.

I almost fell out of my room to present my dishevelled self to the world in the corridor. Jamie saw me and seemed to recognize something familiar in my appearance. He walked straight up to me and said gently, 'Come on, Michael, come and listen to some music.'

In Jamie's room we both sat on the floor after Jamie had put the only record he appeared to own on his turntable. Suddenly, in a volume of noise that I had never experienced before, some appropriate words blasted into an ear-splitting sound: 'When I find myself in times of trouble . . . there will be an answer . . . Let it be, let it be.'

'The Beatles, Jamie,' I said, relieved that the shatteringly loud sound had come to an end.

'Of course,' he said, 'now this time close your eyes.'

I didn't want to upset his good intentions, so I lay back against the wall and waited to be bombarded.

The music seemed even louder this time. I thought my eardrums were going to burst. However, I noticed one small advantage in this deafening exercise. While the music was playing, my mind was protected from any form of distracting thought, including 'have I still got a hangover?'

After the first repeat, I scrambled to my feet, thanked Jamie, who was about to restart the turntable, and disappeared into the now welcome peace and quiet of the passage outside.

I stood for a moment, pleased to realize my hearing had not been permanently impaired. I heard the shuffle of feet on the concrete. I saw it was the slim, retiring figure of Paul, dressed in his usual modest grey v-neck sweater and grey trousers. Paul, with a book clasped to his side, must be on his way to his favourite chair in the common room. He seemed to retreat to that room for most of his waking hours. It must give his timid mind some sanctuary. As he walked slowly past, we gave each other a reassuring and understanding look that said much more than the spoken word.

As I continued to stand not far from Jamie's door, to my surprise I noticed a tall man open the door of the room next to mine and go inside. I knew this room had been empty for months. I felt certain that this man must be a new guest.

I felt it was time to investigate. For some reason I thought it was my right to know everything that was to know about my immediate neighbour.

I tucked some of my shirt into the top of my trousers, walked up to the door next to mine and knocked.

'Come in,' said a deep commanding voice.

I went in, and said in a matter-of-fact manner, 'Hullo, I'm Michael. I live next door.'

'Nice to meet you,' he said, giving me a firm handshake. 'I'm Henry Henning.'

Henry was at least three inches taller than me, and looked to be a good six foot. He was a fine figure of a man with dark brown receding hair, brown eyes and clearly good-looking.

I thought he was about forty-five years of age. What puzzled me was, was there inside all those smart clothes of his a body needing hospital treatment? He looked perfectly fit to me, indeed too fit to ask.

Henry turned his back to me and said in his deep, strong voice. 'I want to change a few clothes, but please don't leave, Michael.'

I then got a shock. As Henry took off his tweed jacket he revealed a strip of leather resting on his white shirt, stretching from his right shoulder to his left hip. He seemed to unbuckle it from the front and then, to my alarm, he dropped a holster and revolver on to his bed!

'Don't worry, it's not loaded,' he said, casually. 'I keep the ammunition elsewhere.'

I was amazed. How could a new patient walk into St Matthew's Hospital for the mentally ill carrying a gun, and not get stopped? I thought about Sam for a moment, and realized that he must not know about it. He might well use it. Perhaps, I considered, Henry was not a new patient after all, but a new type of strong-armed nurse. I could imagine Dr Khan saying, 'Stay away from Mary-Anne, or nurse Henning will make sure you need surgery!'

'Henry,' I asked cautiously, 'are you in here as a patient?'

'Of course,' he said with a slight smile, 'then I want to get back to my job.' He noticed the bewildered expression on my face and helped the situation by saying, 'Oh, you are worried about my revolver. Well, I wear it for my work. I'm a professional bodyguard, but that is all I can say.'

I then wondered whose body did he guard, his or someone else's, and why? Only time would tell, as Henry's lips were now sealed on this matter. I left Henry to complete his unpacking, but agreed to meet him for a stroll round the property after lunch.

When the time came, I showed Henry such contrasting sights as the large swimming pool and the small, eerie cell at the end of the corridor. He was cheerful and interested, but what seemed strange to me was that he was only prepared to talk about me and not himself. I also noticed his eyes were watching me for most of the time. He made me feel slightly uncomfortable. I was not used to such close attention, except from Mary-Anne. I still had not worked out what Henry was suffering from. Maybe he caused nervous disorders in other people, I thought again, but more kindly. Perhaps he behaved as he did simply because he liked me.

I had hoped to see Mary-Anne today, but hospital segregation rules and my new-found friendly shadow made it impossible. Although I could not physically see Mary-Anne, my mind could always present a picture of her to me in a variety of ways. Perhaps she would be looking radiantly beautiful in her black ballgown, or maybe glowing with love and excitement while lying in the gentle sunlight beneath our beech tree. Mary-Anne in thought and mind was always part of me.

3.

I had received a message that I was to be in Dr Khan's consulting room by nine o'clock that morning. What could he want to see me about now, I muttered to myself as I hopped on one foot while trying to get a thin brown sock onto the other cold foot. I was soon dressed, but not pleased to be summoned to see the middle-aged 'mind reader' who might well have conjured up another form of his 'yet to be tested on guinea pigs' therapies.

I shuffled down the corridor with no great enthusiasm towards Dr Khan's door. I realized, however, that even at my slow speed of travel I would not avoid an eventual arrival.

Dr Khan hollered me into his room after hearing some feeble knocking. I had hoped he would not have heard me.

'Ah, Michael, close the door and take a seat.' He had a photograph frame on the edge of his desk, and I noticed from my very low chair that my view of the brown skin, dark eyes and immaculately greased black hair was partly obscured. A psychiatrist's trick to make his patient feel inadequate, I thought grimly.

'Michael,' he said sharply, then decided to say no more while getting up from his chair and walking over to stand beside me.

'Michael,' he said again, with a slight indication of pleasure on his face. 'You have a visitor today. Your wife will be here to see you at about two o'clock.'

'What are you saying?' I retorted, feeling absolutely shocked. 'I haven't got a wife!'

Dr Khan had one hand on the back of the chair and continued to look down upon me from one side; he spoke firmly and clearly as he said, 'You have been married for five years to a young lady called Clare. In fact you have been darn lucky. In the state you must have been in five years ago, you could have married absolutely anybody! As it is, you have landed yourself with a sensible lady.'

'I don't believe you,' I said, noticing a tremor in my hands and a feeling of weakness coming over me.

'Well, once you have met her your memory will

44

improve. I didn't realize you had blanked Clare off completely, or I would have talked about her before.'

I felt in a terrible state. Suddenly my small world, which I could just cope with, had acquired enormous complications. What was I going to do, I thought helplessly?

'Stand up, Michael, and walk across the room,' commanded Dr Khan. I obeyed and wobbled through about six paces before being saved from a fall by placing a trembling hand on the wall.

'This won't do at all with a visitor today. Take two of these sedative tablets,' he said, showing me two small pink pills in the palm of a brown hand and offering me a glass of water at the same time.

'Good, now you can go, but stay near your room so that Clare can find you,' said Dr Khan as though nothing had happened.

I went out of his room readily, and decided to get back to my room and think through this alarming news. In the corridor I saw Sam coming my way. Not now, Sam, I thought. Please don't say what you always do. There was no stopping him. As he passed me, he said guardedly, 'Got a gun, Michael?'

'No, Sam,' I said firmly, continuing to walk slowly, but added in an inaudible voice, 'I know someone who has!'

In the quiet of my room I laid on top of my made bed and breathed heavily. What was I going to do, I thought? What was Clare like, other than being a 'sensible lady'? I knew that the strength of my feelings for Mary-Anne could not be broken by anything, not even the blurred picture of a person called Clare that was forming in my mind.

After a difficult lunch, with Henry questioning me the whole time about my ability to spill so much food, how pale my face was and could he do something to help, I walked slowly into the corridor and down to my door. I decided not to go in – I needed to pace a little.

I turned and started to retrace my steps. Suddenly, from behind me I heard a patter of little shoes on the concrete and a child's voice calling loudly, 'Daddy! Daddy! Daddy!'

I swung round and saw coming towards me a small

three or four-year-old boy, arms outstretched, running towards me at top speed. He had a familiar mop of brown hair, a smart blue button-up overcoat, white socks and buckled brown shoes. He was very happy and excited.

I got down on one knee to be nearer his height. In his enthusiasm he jumped on to me, and his little hands and arms gripped me round the neck. I held him up in front of me and looked into his bright, twinkling eyes.

'David, David,' I said. I knew he was mine as I hugged him and just let tears roll helplessly and freely down my face. How could I have forgotten about this oh so precious little chap?

I knew David was mine because his emotions told me that he was part of me, but where had he been and for how long? Was he happy? My head was buzzing with unanswered questions. Did he understand why I was shut away in another world, I thought to myself? And looking at this fresh-faced, lively young man I wondered if I'd ever be a real father to my son.

As I glanced up I saw through my eyes, their sight blurred with tears, standing in front of me was a short lady with straight, dark hair. She had fine black eyebrows and kind grey eyes. I knew this lady was Clare, but somehow I did not know her at all.

I stood up with David by my side and looked in bewilderment at this small, pretty, almost oriental face. There was love and tenderness in her eyes and she lent forward and kissed me gently on the lips.

'How are you feeling, Michael?' she said in a caring voice.

'Clare,' I said slowly, as it was a person and name that I did not feel used to. 'Clare, I am confused, let's go outside and talk.'

'Whatever you like, Michael,' she said politely. Then she kindly dried my tears with her handkerchief.

David's little hand held on to two of the fingers of my left hand, while Clare gently gripped my right hand. We walked at a leisurely pace through the main doors and out to the sunlit footpath. There were red geraniums growing in the bed next to the building which were a similar colour to Clare's coat and shoes. Indeed, Clare

46

looked very smart and tidy. There was a convenient bench at the endge of the path which all three of us sat on.

Clare said in a cheerful voice, 'David and I have driven for three hours to come and see you. We miss you terribly, you know. The doctor told me you are not ready for a visit back home to Norfolk yet, so tell me how you are.'

'Well,' I said, pausing for thought. 'I am very pleased to see you. David has grown,' I added, guessing. I looked to my left, and the special beech tree caught my eye. I'm not going to mention Mary-Anne today, I thought carefully. One day I might tell her, but Clare seemed a kind person, not the type you are prepared to hurt.

'Clare,' I confessed, 'you won't believe this but I had almost forgotten I had you and David. I think it happened because of all the pills and the treatments they have been giving me. How old is David?' I asked casually as he stood on my thighs and pulled my shirt collar.

'Four,' said Clare, looking rather surprised.

'You go to your Mummy,' I said to David as I passed him across to Clare.

'Let's walk on the golf course,' I said a moment later. 'David might like to run about.'

'Very well,' said Clare, who seemed to genuinely want to please me. We walked onto the grass, Clare turned to me and asked, 'Why do you keep staring at me?'

'Well,' I said, taken aback, 'I haven't seen you for so long. I'd forgotten how pretty you are.'

'Come here, my poor, thin, pale husband,' she said, smiling and grabbing my arm and giving me a peck on the cheek. 'You won't forget about me again, will you, darling?'

'No, I won't, I definitely won't,' I said, frowning and feeling tired and unsteady on my feet.

'Daddy, there is a funny man over there,' David called out, pointing in the direction of Joe, who was about to attack another flowerbed. 'Why does he wear funny clothes?'

'He is a Scout, David,' I said worriedly. I was beginning to feel embarrassed that young David was seeing too much of my strange home. I decided in my confused mind that it was my wish that he would go through life without ever being mentally ill or being aware of the pain suffered by so many such patients. He must be a player on the stage of life, totally preoccupied by a part he enjoyed.

At this point I said to Clare, 'We must go back to my room.'

Clare very obligingly said, 'Yes, whatever you want, darling.'

We walked back on to the path, still arm in arm, with David running and jumping a few yards ahead. I thought of how often I had walked this way, holding Mary-Anne's hand. I felt gently and kindly cared for as I strolled with Clare, and grateful for her loving company. However, the magic, the excitement, the strength of mind and un-predictability of action that I had grown to enjoy with Mary-Anne were all missing.

Back in my room I sat on the bed with David, who took the opportunity to swing his small white-socked legs up and down. Clare quietly and efficiently tidied up my small room, finishing by carefully folding my pyjamas from off the floor and placing them neatly on my pillow.

Clare then sat beside me briefly, saying regretfully, 'Darling, I must take David back now. We have a long way to go.' Then, taking another look at me, she said sympathetically, 'Cheer up, darling,' as she rubbed her hand against the back of my shirt. 'David and I want you to come home soon, more than anything in the world. David, give Daddy a kiss, we will see him again soon.' A wet but meaningful kiss was pressed on my cheek; a hug and a gentle, well-practised lipstick peck, which felt emotionless to me, came with every good wish from Clare.

Once left alone again in my room, I shook a little after the strain of the day's events. I thought about Clare. She was pretty, kind and well-meaning, and seemed to love me in a matter-of-fact sort of way. However, she reminded me that she was a well person from the outside world looking in on me. Mary-Anne and I had so much more in common. We shared our 'home' and felt a silent empathy for each other's difficulties. As I lay back and closed my eyes to sleep, in a haze of confusion I knew that I liked Clare and would not ever want to hurt her or our child, but fate had decreed in my mind that I follow and love

Mary-Anne as no other human being for the rest of my life.

5

1.

The time had come for the Air Vice-Marshal to leave. He thought he had been through an adequate annual drying-out period, and now felt able to face his familiar battle between his wife and the whisky bottle. He gave me a smile and a friendly wave as he carried his case out of the main entrance.

I decided to myself that it was all very well for the Air Vice-Marshal: he knew on arrival at St Matthews when he would be discharged. I had no idea when it would be my turn, but I was certain that I was not prepared to go anywhere without Mary-Anne.

I had not seen Mary-Anne for several days, indeed not since Clare and David's visit. I needed to see Mary-Anne, to talk to her and hold her. I wanted an injection of her almost electric vitality for life. I found if I did not see her for a week or so I became a sad and unhappy man.

However, it always gave me some reassurance to know that we lived in the same 'home', and that our rooms were only a hundred yards apart. Time passed at St Matthews slowly and quietly. I would often console myself by saying, 'I might see Mary-Anne tomorrow.' I didn't know what day of the week it was, as all the days seemed very similar unless I had been fortunate enough to see Mary-Anne.

After another of those quiet empty days, I curled up in my bed and pretended Mary-Anne was with me as I waited for the night's sedatives to assist me to sleep. I imagined my arms were holding her as she lay beside me. I could kiss her attractive smiling face, and press my body against hers and feel its warmth. I wondered if she giggled when she made love; was that my final parting thought for the day?

The next morning I sat up in bed to find, to my horror, that my arms felt numb and I could not move them or my hands. Very alarmed, I swung my legs onto the floor and wondered what on earth had happened to me. I stood up and started to bang on the bottom of the floor with my foot. I called out, 'Graham, help me.'

Fortunately Staff Nurse Graham did arrive fairly quickly. He opened the door and looked annoyed because I had been creating a noise that he felt was unnecessary. 'What's the matter with you?'

'I can't use my arms,' I said, standing rather helplessly in front of him.

Graham seemed to know what to do immediately. He lifted up one of my arms and held my hand in front of him. Then, with his other hand he pulled a large pin from the lapel of his white coat. With quick precision he pushed the pin into my hand in three or four places. I could see a little blood, but felt nothing.

Graham realized that I could feel nothing in either arm, and that I was unable to control them. He looked at my concerned face and said, 'Don't worry, Michael. It's just a problem with your nerves. They should come back in a few days.' He kindly helped me to dress and then set me forth down the passage towards the dining room.

I thought carefully as I sauntered up the corridor with my limp arms dangling by my side. Why should nerves stop me using my arms? What nerves? Which part of my body would go numb next? Was I worried about something? Yes I was! Right now, what would Mary-Anne say about her previously inadequate boyfriend? She could take my trousers down in a manic moment and laugh at my hairy legs. I couldn't stop her.

In the dining room I was soon reminded that I had more immediate mundane problems, like eating. I stepped over a bench and sat down next to Jamie. I looked at the bowl of prunes and the plate of toast and butter. I felt quite hungry. Probably all the more so because I seemed to be looking at forbidden fruit. Jamie eventually turned to me with a mouthful of toast and managed to emit the words, 'I'm getting confirmed today.'

'But you have not been Christened,' I said, a little surprised.

'Oh, they are doing that at the same time.'

'Good,' I said, with little feeling.

'If you don't want your prunes, I'll have them,' said Jamie in his usual unobservant but likeable manner.

'Jamie, look at me,' I said crossly. 'My bloody arms won't work.'

'I'm sorry,' apologized Jamie. 'I didn't know. Look, I'll spoon the prunes in, and you spit the stones out. Here goes.'

As Jamie kindly spooned the prunes into my mouth, I became a completely helpless target for his sense of humour.

'Had a bad night with Mary-Anne, then?' he said, chuckling to himself and quickly spooning in another prune to block a reply. 'Did she get a bit rough?' he continued, laughing. 'I don't suppose she broke anything else?'

I spat out a whole prune and said firmly, 'Jamie, I don't damn well know why I can't move my arms! Graham thinks it's nerves or something.'

'Well, I'm really sorry,' said Jamie, being serious for a moment, and then he had to comment, 'Mary-Anne will be upset.'

'She will understand,' I said, trying to hear an echo of hope in the tone of my own voice.

Manners when eating were varied, and different techniques were ignored by other patients. However, Henry, who was sitting opposite to us, did eventually notice my unusual handicap.

'Michael, why can't you use your arms?' he asked sympathetically.

'Henry, I simply don't know,' I replied loudly.

I turned to Jamie, whose long hair did give him a more saintly appearance than the rest of us, even though it must have impaired his vision at times.

'Jamie, how about a slice of buttered toast?' I said optimistically.

'I'll feed him,' said Henry eagerly.

'No, you can't reach, I'll do it,' said Jamie, scraping soft

52

butter over the black ash surface of the chosen piece of toast.

After crunching what I could of the toast course, just avoiding Jamie's fingers, I was helped to wash the remains down with a cold cup of tea.

I swung my legs back over the bench and turned round towards Jamie before leaving the dining room. I felt a need to 'pull Jamie's leg' after all his digs at me about Mary-Anne, when I was unable to speak.

'Jamie,' I said, getting his attention, 'remember when you get Christened today you will have to go through the usual ritual for adults of being totally immersed in cold water. I should wear a bathing cap if I were you!'

'That's not right!' said Jamie, objecting to such a possibility, but at the same time looking rather concerned.

Out in the passage I found Henry had come to join me. 'I'll be your arms for a while,' he said, not waiting no for an answer.

'Thank you, Henry,' I said, not sure what invitation I had accepted.

At that moment Dr Khan walked up to me, obviously already informed by Graham that Michael's arms were out of order. He did not look pleased, as if to imply that this was another of my self-inflicted failings which had appeared solely to bother him. He lifted one of my arms casually and then let it swing back into position. At the end of this thirty-second medical examination he said in a couldn't-care-less sort of way, 'It may be as a result of hypertension.' Then, to my extreme surprise, 'I want you to go swimming, now!'

I started to say, 'But how can I swim without arms,' but he had already turned and walked away.

Henry carried my towel and swimming shorts to the pool. He also helped me change, which I did not like, but could not avoid.

'Stay up the shallow end,' Henry advised.

'Perhaps my arms will float,' I said, and then reflected that it was unlikely.

I managed the steps into the shallow end, balancing very carefully on each step. Henry meanwhile had dived into the deep end, where there were about ten other people enjoying themselves, swimming and splashing about.

My feet on the bottom, I walked very slowly up the pool until the water came up to my chest. I stood there feeling desperately upset and helpless. As I looked at all the fit people doing what I could normally do, I wept tears of self-pity into the water. I decided all I could attempt was to kick with my feet and lie on my back. I leant backwards and paddled my legs and feet. My arms were still useless and just hung down pointing at the bottom of the pool. In a very few moments my head was under the water and my legs, without the aid of my arms, had propelled my body, still on its back, to the blue concrete base of the swimming pool.

I lay flat, unable to get up, and looked for a few seconds through the water at the light above. The obvious thought flashed through my mind: Michael, you will drown in just a moment, and there is nothing you can do to save yourself.

Suddenly there was a big splash, and before I knew it the strong arms of my 'bodyguard' had brought me to the surface, spluttering and coughing. This strong, fit man in his forties, 'Henry with the gun', had saved my life. After a few minutes of lying on the tiles at the edge of the pool I was able to talk.

'Thank you Henry, let's get dressed,' I said quietly, still shocked by the incident and not really sure what to say.

As we walked back to my room I questioned Henry. 'Why do you think Dr Khan insisted I went swimming? Was it because he wanted me to drown, or was there some therapeutic value in trying to swim with no arms that I had missed out on?'

'I really don't know,' said Henry, who was equally puzzled by Dr Khan. 'Perhaps Dr Khan felt that if he put you in a situation where you absolutely had to use your arms, you would do so and break the "spell,"' he said rather unbelievingly, and added, 'Well, if that was the case it didn't work.'

Lunch was a struggle, but with Henry's patient help I had something to eat. As I looked at Henry helping me, I wondered why I had been so concerned and suspicious about the amount of attention he seemed to be paying me when he first arrived. He seemed a genuinely caring person who enjoyed my company, even if it had its physical problems at the moment.

Why, I thought, was Henry at St Matthews at all? He seemed mentally well. I decided not to ask him. I was just pleased to have him around and I tried not to think about his revolver.

In the afternoon we met Jamie, thoroughly Christened and confirmed and looking delighted with himself. 'I'm discharged! Now I can go back to London,' he said in a high-spirited voice.

We wished him good luck as he went to collect his clothes, his guitar and, no doubt, his all-important record. What would happen to Jamie, I asked myself, when he got back to the music and drug scene he knew so well? Would it be all music?

Standing near the main entrance, I said to Henry, 'There is a lady I simply must go and see.'

'You mean Mary-Anne, the tall curly blonde with a pretty face?' he replied immediately.

'Yes,' I said after a pause, having not heard this casual observer's description of her before. 'Henry, it's raining outside, so there is a very good chance that she is in her room. I'm fed up with the segregation rules. If a staff nurse is looking for me, tell him you last saw me walking in the rain or something,' I pleaded breathlessly.

'Don't worry about a thing,' said Henry in a composed manner. 'I'm good at concocting alibis.'

I wandered off, hoping that I would look invisible in the ladies' area. The ladies themselves would never give me away, but any form of doctor or nurse was a different matter. As it was, I reached Mary-Anne's door at the top of the stairs without any problems. I tapped the toe of a shoe against the bottom of her door, which opened almost immediately.

'Oh, it's you, Michael,' Mary-Anne said, smiling. 'How did you get here?'

'I flew,' I replied flippantly. She discretely closed the door, then put her arms round me and gave me a soft, prolonged kiss on my cheek.

'Is there something wrong with me? Don't you want to hug me today?' she said, a little upset.

I looked straight into her beautiful blue eyes and said, as though it was a British Rail platform announcement, 'I am not able to use or feel my arms today. I hope it will not be many days before I'm able to hug you as I would like to do most of the time.'

'Oh dear!' she said, realizing she was now dealing with even faultier goods than she had first suspected. 'You had better sit down,' she said, pointing to a small wooden chair and placing herself on her side on the bed, with a hand propping up her head.

I was sitting close enough to Mary-Anne to see some of the ingredients of that sparkling magic that followed me wherever I went.

'You look beautiful,' I said, with feeling.

'Thank you,' she said, smiling again, and went on to say, 'you are not so bad yourself. Pity about the arms. You look as though you are being held up by a coathanger.' Then she laughed heartily. I felt she cared about my predicament, and so she did the only thing she knew she did so well, and that was to cheer me up.

'They will get better soon, won't they?' she asked through her laughter.

'Of course,' I said with blind confidence, not daring to suggest that she might have to put up with me like this for much longer.

There was a moment of quiet while I continued to look at the lady I loved so much, and wondered to myself where that kind wife Clare fitted into my life. Compared to Mary-Anne, Clare was somebody I hardly knew, somebody from my past life in the outside world. Suddenly, almost surprising myself, I said boldly, 'Are you married, Mary-Anne?' and added, 'Not that it really matters.' You would have thought from her immediate reaction, which was to curl up on the bed and to roll about in unrestrained convulsive laughter, that I had just cracked the funniest joke she had ever heard.

'Me married!' she said indignantly, but still giggling. 'I don't want a husband, a house, a job or even babies. I want to stay free and wild. I want to keep getting a big buzz out of life as I do with people like you.'

Why didn't she say 'a person like you', or better still, simply, 'with you', I thought to myself? I couldn't stop her having other men friends any more than anybody could stop her from doing anything she wanted. However, I desperately needed, in order to justify my existence as worthwhile, a special permanently reserved piece of her affectionate heart and mind, just for me. I persuaded myself that this was indeed the case, and that my relationship with Mary-Anne was unique and untouchable.

My thoughts were broken by Mary-Anne saying, 'You know, Michael, I saw you from the window walking with a young lady in a red coat yesterday. Was it your mother?' she said with a twinkle in her eye.

I grinned and said, 'Yes, one of them!' We both laughed as I moved beside the bed, knelt down and kissed her firmly and lovingly on her lips.

2.

Ten days later I was sitting on my bed in the evening, my arms still useless, when Dr Khan came hurriedly into my room. He looked angry as he said abruptly, 'Stand up, Michael, show me these arms.' He then proceeded to have a tug-of-war session with each arm. He pulled them and bent them in every direction possible, while saying with a grimace, 'There is absolutely nothing wrong with these arms.'

When Dr Khan took a breather from his fight with my arms, I realized straight away that I now had a sense of feeling in my hands. I tried to lift my arms, and to my joy and amazement I found I could. I smiled with happiness and delight as I continued to wave my hands above my head.

Although Dr Khan had sorted out my problem, he did not wait for my thanks but left with the same haste that he had arrived with.

All I could think of doing was telling the whole hospital my good news. I skipped up the corridor, waving my arms in the air. I opened Henry's door and said to him, 'Look, my arms work!'

'That's marvellous,' he said. 'You will be able to swim and eat. How were they cured?'

'Would you believe Dr Khan broke the spell with brute force?' I replied excitedly.

'Why didn't he do it before?' questioned Henry.

'I have no idea,' I said. 'Perhaps there's a full moon tonight!'

I went to bed that night a relieved and happy man. I even enjoyed putting my pyjamas on. Most of my friends and, hopefully, Mary-Anne would have heard my good news by now. I closed my eyes and thought, tomorrow I will really celebrate.

When Doris came into my room in the morning for the paper ritual, I noticed her curly hair was no longer red but had received a devastating blue dye, which was not a subtle colour if she intended it to look remotely natural. The paper was dropped in its usual place, then Doris paused and pulled a large white envelope out from behind her floral apron. She handed it to me, saying, 'Here you are, dear.'

'Thank you, Doris,' I said as she started to leave, and politely followed with, 'I do like your hair.'

'It makes a change,' she said, smiling her way round towards Henry's room.

I had not received any post for months, so it was with considerable interest that I started to open my white envelope. As I pulled a card from the envelope I realized it was a birthday card! There was a smiling shark swimming on the front with a large cake with pink icing and candles on its nose. 'Somefin tells me it's your Birthday' it said, and inside was written, 'With all my love, Clare,' and a kind squiggle by David. On the back it said, 'Please ring me, Drillingham 4475, sometime.'

'It's my birthday!' I exclaimed, 'And my arms are better. We are going to celebrate today!' I dressed quickly, and then managed to sit next to Henry for breakfast.

'Henry, it's my birthday, and I'm inviting you to come out with Mary-Anne and me for a drink at "The George" tonight.'

'But three's a crowd,' said Henry. 'I haven't got a girlfriend.'

'Don't worry about that,' I said confidently, 'I'll get you a girlfriend after breakfast.' Henry didn't know what I was talking about, and looked sceptical as he carried on eating.

On our way back from the dining room I was lucky to meet Sylvia, who was often off her own territory and was a useful messenger. Sylvia was desperately overweight, poor thing, to the extent that running presented a serious physical problem. She was quite short and displayed a plump babyface smile most of the time.

'Sylvia, be a friend,' I said pleadingly, 'and ask Mary-Anne to come to "The George" with me tonight. Tell her I'll meet her at the main doors at eight o'clock.'

'Okay,' said Sylvia, still smiling above her ample chins.

'Well, you are fixed up. What wizard plan have you got for me?' asked Henry. The messenger had gone on her way, so it was safe for Henry to make one thing quite clear. 'I am not going out with Sylvia,' he said firmly.

'No, of course not. Come with me,' I said, walking towards Staff Nurse Graham.

'Graham, please may I make a quick telephone call on your phone in the nurses' room?' I said, being as polite as possible.

'Yes, I'll take you to it, but you had better be quick.'

Henry stood beside me with Graham near the door as I lifted the phone. I dialled 100. The operator answered and said, 'Can I help you?' The ideal kind, well-spoken young voice that I needed, I thought to myself.

'Yes,' I replied, 'would you like to come out for a drink with me this evening? I am a six-foot, good-looking psychology student called Henry,' I said, looking at Henry, who by now had a 'please don't do this' expression on his face.

'Yes, all right, my name is Dawn,' she said, with the same off-hand manner that she would have used to give me a telephone number.

'Lovely,' I said, 'I'll see you at "The George" at Nimbrington at eight-fifteen. You won't miss me. My name is Henry and I'll be standing in the middle of the public bar with an empty pint mug.'

'I'll try not to be late. It would be a shame to leave you with an empty glass!' she said brightly, followed by an earthy, 'See you,' and the dialling tone.

'You are never alone with a phone,' I said, smiling at Henry. 'Dawn will meet you at the pub at 8.15 pm.'

'I don't know at all,' said Henry, looking solemn. 'I've never been on a blind date before. Dawn may look like Sylvia, and anyway, what type of telephonist goes out with anybody who rings up?'

'I don't know, I've never tried it before,' I admitted.

Henry still looked worried and astonished as Graham said clearly to us, 'I could stop all this if I wanted to.'

'Please,' I begged Graham, 'please let us go out this evening. My arms are better, and it's my birthday.'

'How old are you?' he asked.

'I don't know, do you?' I said, finding his question irrelevant to our discussion.

Graham took a deep breath and then said, while exhaling, 'All right, but you must be back by ten o'clock. I'll be waiting for you.'

We left the nurses' room straight away so that Graham could not change his sometimes-not-so-understanding mind.

I selected from my limited wardrobe my only jacket and my second pair of brown corduroy trousers. I looked at my head of hair in the mirror: it stuck up everywhere and would have made a good dusting mop for Doris. I doused it with water, found a parting and hoisted into position a knot in the only tie I owned. The tie itself, a dirty beige, could have passed as a strip of hessian sacking. Never mind, I thought, I did attempt to look as though some effort had been made to improve my appearance, which was not usually the case.

It occurred to me that as it was a quarter to eight I had better check on Henry. He just might be trying to 'chicken out'. I breezed into Henry's room without knocking and saw him standing near his window, dressed immaculately.

'You look very smart, Henry,' I said. 'Are you nearly ready?'

'Ready for a drink, but I'm not sure about Dawn,' commented Henry.

Under his jacket was there a revolver, I wondered? So I said casually, 'You won't be armed tonight, Henry, will you?'

'Of course not,' he said, 'my revolver is in a safe place until I need it.'

Only mildly reassured I walked with Henry to the main door where, to my delight, I found Mary-Anne looking tantalisingly beautiful, if a little over-made-up, waiting for us. I leant forward and kissed her on the cheek. As the three of us set off across the golf course, I admired Mary-Anne's clothes and her style, even though the yellow and white get-up was very familiar to me.

'Mary-Anne, it's my birthday,' I said.

'Great, but I'm even more pleased about your arms,' she said, turning to smile at me. 'Did you get a card from mother?' she said with an obvious wink.

'Yes, from one of them!' I said, smiling.

I decided to bring Henry into the conversation. He looked lost and apprehensive, in spite of his extremely smart clothes.

'Don't you think Henry would make any young lady happy this evening, Mary-Anne?' I said, as we strode in the cool of the evening over the soft green grass. Then I added, 'A young lady called Dawn is going to meet him at the pub.'

'Don't talk about her, Michael,' said Henry firmly. 'I bet she has got two heads, bloodshot eyes, and eats men for breakfast.'

'So Dawn's a blind date,' said Mary-Anne, 'do I know her?'

'Unlikely, unless you make trunk calls,' I said, smiling at Henry, and got a less than happy expression in reply.

Mary-Anne giggled her way into the public bar and we followed. The room was half full already, but there was a small round table with four chairs near the bar, which was ideal for us. Mary-Anne, who seemed to be winding up into a particularly happy mood, sat down and at the same time handed me a five pound note, saying, 'I'll buy this round, if you will get them.' Mary-Anne, I thought, is nearly as generous with her money as she is with her emotions.

This seemingly simple act of buying three drinks proved a problem because Henry said, 'I'm supposed to have an empty pint mug.'

'Well you had better start with a full one,' I insisted.

We sat round our table, with Henry facing the door. I couldn't understand if Henry was terrified of women or, more likely, just preferred men. I felt he was forcing himself to be polite about the situation in front of Mary-Anne and myself.

I was enjoying my beer, and indeed was soon on my second pint. Henry, a slower drinker, commented to me, 'Michael, you ought to arrange for a pipe from the draught beer barrel to run from here to your room.'

'It wouldn't be the same, Henry. I enjoy the pub atmosphere,' I said, smiling, thinking what a splendid idea, but unfortunately not feasible.

Just then Mary-Anne said, 'I bet that is her!' encouraging us all to look towards the door. There, wiggling her little bottom in a pair of skintight jeans and excessively high-heeled black shoes, paraded a small, smiling eighteen-or-nineteen-year-old girl. She had a well-proportioned figure that she was clearly proud of, dark curly hair and a pretty face with a generous coating of make-up.

'Good heavens,' said Henry, 'is this Dawn?'

'Only one way to find out,' I said casually, and squeezed Mary-Anne's hand under the table. 'Drink the rest of your pint and then stand up in the middle of the room displaying your six feet of good looks,' I instructed Henry with a positive voice, although he looked as though if he knew of a back entrance he would use it.

The tight jeans, frilly white low-cut blouse and high heels that must have required a balancing act, wiggled, wobbled and glowed from the face in our direction. I held up Henry's empty glass and pointed at him. There was an immediate response. The young lady waved and started to weave her neat little body between the tables and chairs towards us. On her way, one young man smacked her bottom and called out, 'Alroyt, darlin'?' She was quite unperturbed, and turned and gave the chap a peck of bright red lipstick on the cheek.

Arriving at our table, with most of the men in the pub

looking at us, she said, 'Which one of you is Henry with the lovely deep voice?'

'It's this chap here,' I said, putting my hand on Henry's shoulder and trying to raise the pitch of my voice.

'Oh Henry, aren't you smashing,' she said, smiling at him and moving round to put her arms round his neck as if to claim him.

Henry's immediate reaction was to stand up, which made him look twice the height of the young lady. 'Dawn, is it?' asked Henry, offering his hand.

'Yes, why, were you expecting someone else?' she said cockily.

With perfect manners, Henry put his hand away and said, 'I did not know who to expect, but now I've met you I'm delighted you answered my invitation. What would you like to drink?'

'Rum and Coke please, handsome,' she said, trying to rub the palm of her hand on the small piece of exposed shirt next to his tie.

Henry completed the round and we all sat at our small table, with me hoping that at last I could talk to Mary-Anne while Henry consumed the dubious delights of Dawn. However, at that moment Mary-Anne had other ideas. She drank down a full glass of gin and tonic as though it was water, and then stood up, pushing her chair out of the way with her legs, and started to sing in her operatic soprano the words to 'Happy Birthday'. Within seconds the thirty or so other customers joined in, but when it came to 'Dear Michael,' my name was an enthusiastic muddled confusion of noise. Many people shouted 'speech'. I said hurriedly to Mary-Anne, 'I can't make a speech!'

'You will have to say something, and quickly,' she said through a slightly stifled laugh.

Given courage, which I didn't think I normally had, from my evening of imbibing, I stood up and faced the happy crowd who were just poised to laugh at me. I spoke clearly but cautiously, telling the only joke that occurred to me.

'The other day I came into this pub with my miniature white poodle on a lead. When I got to the bar, the landlord said, "Dogs are not allowed in here." I said, "But mine is a guide dog!" The landlord exclaimed, "But guide dogs are usually big dogs like Alsatians or Labradors." "Why, what have they given me?"'

There was some chuckling and good-hearted laughter. Then one outspoken man felt the need to shout out, 'Where's your poodle now?'

Without thinking I said, 'She's wearing a white blouse and drinking a gin and tonic.' I tried to look towards Mary-Anne without her noticing. The man laughed. I sat down, hoping my little joke at her expense had not offended her.

Mary-Anne smiled at me, and to my surprise said, holding my hand, 'But I'm not on a lead tonight,' and giggled happily.

'Oh yes you are, my love,' was my instant reply. 'I want you to stay with me.'

At this stage we seemed to have a spare chair at our table because Dawn had moved her slender body on to Henry's lap where, as I'm sure she would have said, she was just getting to know him. Henry himself seemed to have been caressed into an early phase of sleep.

I stumbled to the bar, thinking one more beer wouldn't matter, when Mary-Anne called from the table, 'You have got two here.' I put up my hand and returned to enjoy sinking two pints from some well-wishers.

I looked at my watch, which seemed to have been hiding up my sleeve. It was either ten minutes to midnight or it was ten o'clock. Either way was not good news. I staggered to my feet and said, 'Come on, you lot, you have all had enough to drink.'

'Speak for yourself,' said Mary-Anne quietly.

Henry had woken up a bit and was looking after Dawn. He lifted her up with effortless ease and put her on her shoeless feet. Mary-Anne led the way to the door. I had a distinct problem in trying to walk normally, but with the help of my guide we arrived outside in the fresh air. Henry was behind me, but there was no Dawn.

'You've lost Dawn,' I said to him as I held on to Mary-Anne's shoulder for support.

'I know,' said Henry. 'I've left her working her way

round all the men in the pub. She's a nice girl, but a complete nymphomaniac; likes anything in trousers and is not too fussy. I feel quite relieved,' he said, smiling, and added with some urgency, 'Let's get back home before Graham strings us up.' He was also certainly thinking, don't give Dawn the chance to follow.

After re-routing our return journey across the golf course into a somewhat longer, often indirect, stumbled walk, I hugged Mary-Anne so hard that I must have nearly crushed her bones.

Henry and I strolled in the direction of our rooms when suddenly, out in the dimly-lit corridor we bumped into an angry, noisy Graham.

'I said ten o'clock. What sort of time do you think this is?' he shouted at us.

In my uninhibited stupor, I held on to Graham's coat and said, 'You are making far too much noise, old chap. There are people here trying to get some sleep.'

Graham stormed off, saying loudly as he went, 'I'll be back in five minutes, and you had both better be in bed by then.'

One last problem faced me. I found that my excessive intake of beer had caused me to lose my judgement when trying to turn corners. I made several attempts to turn in through the open door into my room, only to find I fell over at the crucial moment. Eventually, Henry kindly dragged me in and dumped me on the bed. Henry left for his room while I held firmly onto the bedside table, the only object that appeared to stay still in my room. I vowed that I would never have another drink in my life, and I prayed that sleep would soon overtake me.

6

The next morning the sun may have been shining, but I did not notice. It was nine-thirty, and I was already half an hour late for a group therapy meeting. Without bothering to dress, I appeared unshaven and in my pyjamas in the common room, where a circle of bored faces were attempting to listen to Dr Khan.

Dr Khan was not pleased to see me. He abruptly instructed a staff nurse to give me a cold shower and some black coffee to cure whatever might have been wrong with me.

I soon felt well awake, if a little sad and reticent as I tried to adjust to a normal day in my life which did not include beer or Mary-Anne.

In the dining room at lunchtime I was correctly dressed, well-shaven and still full of black coffee. The room seemed filled with hungry patients, most of whom I did not know. I thought that it was shepherd's pie that I was about to eat. It was difficult to be certain. I wanted the salt pot but I could not reach it, and there was no-one sitting opposite me. So I stood up, with the back of my knees pressed against the bench, and started to lean across the table with my right arm outstretched. To my surprise I felt extremely giddy, my vision blurred and my body, out of control, crashed down in an unconscious state on top of the plates, bowls and glasses that decked the table.

I next found myself sitting in a wheelchair, attended by a nurse, parked outside the dining room, which sounded particularly noisy.

The nurse asked me, 'Do you feel all right now, Michael?'

'Yes, thank you,' I said, a little uncertain of the truth of my reply.

'Right,' the nurse said, letting off the brake. 'I will take you to your room where you can lie down for a bit.'

I rested on my bed for an hour or so when a large, tall, male staff nurse, who looked as if he was a part-time wrestler, came into my room.

'Michael Simpson, you are to come with me to another part of the hospital,' he said sternly. He could have added, from his expression, 'If you are any trouble I will break your arm,' but there was no need. I was confused but I had got the message.

While the monster of a man watched me, I placed my few clothes, wash things and birthday card into my small suitcase. Then we set off towards the main doors, with him never more than a few inches away from me.

'Where am I going?' I asked imploringly.

'Just come with me and don't ask questions,' he said firmly.

Left with no choice in the matter, I followed along the tarmac path, occasionally passing another patient. Most meaningful of all was the moment we passed the beech tree. I realized this hulk of a man, with no manners, was taking me away from Mary-Anne.

'Will I soon be allowed back to my room?' I asked anxiously. There was no reply. The nurse's hard, scowling acne-battered face just kept looking straight ahead.

We arrived at a reinforced green metal door at the back of the large brick building known as the Chronic Section of the Hospital. The nurse pressed an obscured bell, and we waited.

I stood thinking to myself. Rumour had it that, once inside this place you could get forgotten about forever and never see the outside world again. I knew that in the female section there was a lady in her sixties who had been there for over forty years. Her only misdemeanour was the frequency with which she would take her knickers off in front of anybody and everybody. I felt this was quite a harmless occupation and did not deserve permanent hospitalization.

Why had I been brought to such a place, I kept asking

67

myself? My only possible error in the eyes of the authorities was the well-known fact that I had fallen in love with another patient. I consoled myself a little with the thought that there must be some mistake in my case.

I heard heavy footsteps approaching the inside of the door, followed by the noise of bolts being moved before the door swung open.

'I've got Michael Simpson,' my nurse said, taking a firm grip on my right arm and looking at his equally well-built colleague who stood in the doorway.

Everything happened very quickly. Each nurse held an arm and practically lifted me bodily down a short passage to a door made up on the outside of metal bars. The door was unlocked with a large key. One nurse held onto my suitcase while the other pushed me into this dark room without comment. There was a loud bang of metal on metal as the door was slammed shut behind me.

I soon realized I was in a cell. A padded one. I banged my fists furiously on the door and yelled, 'Let me out of this bloody place. Have you gone fucking mad? Why am I in this stinking cage?'

No-one came. No-one seemed to hear or care a damn.

In a mood of total rejection, I looked round my cell. The furnishing had definitely been done sparing every expense and comfort. On the floor there was a shabby mattress with blood stains on it and a small bowl which could have had several incompatible uses. 'Only urinate after eating,' I could hear the command. The walls were padded up to six foot and finished in filthy canvas material. The only light came from a small barred window near the ceiling.

Why was I in this hell-hole of a place, and how the devil was I going to get out of it? I asked myself in a state of desperation as I flopped down on the mattress. I had already realized that those nurses had got me in a losing position, whatever I did. If I yell at them and bang the door, they will say, 'Just as well the young pillock is locked away.' If I keep quiet, they will say, 'He must be content in that cell, so we will leave him there.'

Heavy footsteps approached my door. The door was unlocked and flung open. The same two nurses showed

their ugly faces. The acned nurse was carrying a hypo-
dermic syringe with a long needle protruding from it,
complemented by a sickly grin on his face.

He said, 'Jimmy, get his trousers off,' and walked
forward, closing the door.

Jimmy pushed me against a wall, stood in front of me
and shouted, 'Take your trousers off, you bastard, before
I rip them off!'

'Leave me alone, you ugly pervert!' I retorted.

'Dave,' said Jimmy, turning to his pockmarked mate,
'this one is going to need both of us.'

'Right, I'll show the little prick,' said Dave, crossly. 'Pull
him down on the floor.'

I lay face up on the mattress with Jimmy's knee across
my chest. Dave sat on my legs and put the syringe on the
floor beside him, resting it in a crack in the brickwork.

'Right, this will be a pleasure, you up-market ponce,'
said Dave, with an eager grin as his large fingers
unbuttoned my trousers. 'Jimmy, hold the bugger's arms a
minute.' I felt certain that they had perfected this routine
years ago.

Dave pulled off my trousers, chucked them on the floor
and, as if eager to see my body, quickly leant forward and
removed my pants. At this point he paused to stand back
and look at me before saying, 'Pathetic!'

My desperate cry of, 'Leave me alone, you filthy shit!'
was followed by a sharp boot on the side of my leg. The
pain was bad enough, but it did not mask my fears of what
these two creeps were going to try next.

'Roll him over, mate, let's see his bum,' said Dave,
starting to twist my legs. Now face down on the mattress, I
could not move to do anything about Dave's hands which
were slapping and cruelly squeezing my buttocks. When
he felt like it he would allow his fist to punch me between
my legs before returning to pinch and cut the flesh on my
bottom with his long nails.

'God help me, what have I done to deserve this?' I called
out helplessly.

'Shut up!' said Jimmy. 'No-one's going to hurt you.'

As tears came to my eyes I knew it was all too much for
me. I hated this whole damn world! I felt totally distressed

69

and foully forced into submission. I sobbed, then cried hysterically.

Dave took his hand away and said, as though it was out of some sort of twisted kindness, 'I will tell you, soft arse, why you are in this dump. You have become a violent troublemaker. Today you caused the sort of bloody riot in your dining room that we don't stand for round here. Hundreds of bloody plates were smashed, and some patients were hurt.

'Right,' he said purposefully, 'start remembering in your sleep and dream about a battered body – yours!' Then he plunged the needle into a bare buttock. As he forced the fluid into me I was in excruciating pain, and cried out for help in an ear-piercing scream.

As I felt myself regaining consciousness I realized it was night-time from the blackened barred window and the lit electric bulb hanging from the high ceiling. I rubbed my hand on my chest. My shirt had gone. I was completely naked. As I tried to move, my body felt sore and bruised. The full horror of my situation became clear to me.

I knelt on the mattress and slowly tried to stand. I got to my feet quietly and with difficulty. I did not want to hurt my body, which seemed unknown to me, or attract the attention of those evil pigs who had assaulted me.

I struggled round my cell, picking up and putting on my orange shirt, pants, brown trousers, socks and shoes. I felt pleased to be dressed, even if I didn't know for how long I would be.

I sat on the mattress and tried to think of the most pleasant thing I could think of. My beautiful blonde lady giggling and teasing me under the beech tree came kindly and easily to mind. Oh, how I loved Mary-Anne. Alarmed, however, at a dreadful thought, I mouthed the words, 'She will never know of this place.'

Too soon for me, but inevitably, there was a clanking sound as a key threw the lever in my door lock. Dave, who was about as much a nurse as a knacker, entered the cell carrying a small oval tray.

'You're dressed,' he said, not surprised, and handed the tray down to me. A bowl of vegetable soup, bread and milk. I was desperately hungry and ate enthusiastically.

With my mouth half full of bits of soggy vegetables, I asked Dave more politely than he deserved, 'Can I see Dr Khan?'

Dave smiled a winning smile and said, 'Dr Khan is on two weeks' holiday, so I've got you for as long as I want.'

'Is there another doctor I can see?' I pleaded with him.

Dave was prepared for this request, and replied harshly, 'Bad luck, soft arse; none of them know you are here, and I'm not telling them. It is a nursing decision. We run this hospital, and you remember that!'

Dave moved closer to me and put on a slightly softer voice. 'If you co-operate with me you may not need another of those particularly painful paraldehyde jabs. It's not much fun at night with only a corpse in the cell to kick around. Now look, soft arse,' he said, taking a deep breath and pointing a finger at me, 'if you do as you are told and accept just a little physical punishment, which should be a pleasant relief for you and help me pass the time, there will be no more jabs and plenty of food. On the other hand, soft arse,' he said, walking behind me and clipping the top of my head with the palm of his hand, 'if you don't co-operate, I will treat that body of yours as a toy, to be played with and broken!'

I shouted back at his horrible poxy-looking face, 'Let me out of this place. I should not be here,' and added, 'nor should anyone else!' Getting even more angry, but still terrified inside myself of what this foul-minded thug might do next, I made my own demand. 'Let me out now, or as soon as I can, I will tell the hospital director and the police all about you!'

'Soft arse, you are way out of order,' Dave said crossly, and hit me hard with his palm across the side of my head as if to reaffirm his point.

He passed round to the front of me, scratching some inflamed lumps on his face. He looked at me, but avoided meeting my stare. Then he spoke almost casually. 'I'd hate, because of an administration error, to cause that blonde bit of skirt you go around with to have a bumpy night in a cell with my mate. He gets a bit rough, you know, doesn't care what he does.'

'You bastard,' I cried. 'If you ever go near that lady I

71

will kill you!'

Dave laughed at me and then through his fat, ugly smirk said, 'Well, you know what to do. Keep your bloody mouth shut. OK, soft arse?'

'Yes, I promise,' I said, totally humbled by Dave's threat.

The mere thought that this ill-conceived hulk had possibly even seen Mary-Anne, let alone that he could contemplate a wildly crude plan involving her, made me feel sick. I had not realized there were such bastards in this world as Dave. I had always thought of this part of the hospital as a form of prison for people who had committed no crime. It had never occurred to me that it also provided protection and opportunity for habitual criminals such as Dave, a presumably trusted member of the nursing staff.

Dave kicked my leg violently with his seemingly purpose-made boot. I yelled, 'Ow, you bastard!' And then quickly pressed my hands over the pain. Dave looked as though he wanted my complete attention but was obviously incapable of just asking for it. He slowly opened his soft, fat cod-like mouth and started speaking assertively.

'You have two hours in here to think whether to be sensible and co-operate, or whether you are going to make me give you another of those bloody agonising jabs. You don't understand, soft arse. I want you to have a chance to help yourself. I want you to try and stand up for your pathetic self, instead of lying on the mattress blubbering helplessly. Have you ever trodden on a fly, soft arse? Well, it doesn't give you or the fly a thrill, but a bloody bad-tempered hornet, there is a fight on your hands, a really exciting challenge. You find some spunk to fight, and at least you will know what happens to your body. Think about it, soft arse, if you've really got a bloody brain. I'll be back.'

The door slammed and the most revolting inhuman bully that I had ever met had gone. I immediately made an effort to stand up. My limbs hurt in many places, but I managed to walk a few yards and eventually to urinate with some accuracy into the pot-like object in my cell.

I returned to sitting on the blood-stained mattress. I

72

thought, if I was to find anybody strong or mad enough to be capable of beating up Dave, he would not be prepared to fight him. Dave always had to feel certain before he attacked anybody that they had not the slightest chance of winning. On the other hand, his bullying instincts gained no pleasure if there was no contest, because then there was no reward for this strange ego to feed on.

I asked myself the crazy question: was I when unconscious going to allow myself to be battered helplessly to pulp, or was I going to fight and have to look at this ugly animal while he revelled in my pain and inevitable downfall?

As my mind sought for an answer that made any sort of sense out of my predicament, I felt cold. I felt my familiar tremor find its way back into my hands and knees. I was feeling very weak and slightly faint. I lay back on the mattress, closed my eyes and tried, if only for a few minutes, to shut out my horrific, hopeless world.

I was roused by the 'clank' of the door opening and the gross reappearance of Dave. The 'jab or joust' question was no doubt on his lips and about to be poisonously posed again. As I looked at this hateful bully, I vowed to myself that one day I would try to find a way to really hurt him. I wished that I could expose this torturing coward for what he was, but Mary-Anne would be at risk.

'Michael,' Dave said, politely, 'Dr Wandless wants to see you in his office upstairs. I have got your case. Would you like to come with me?'

I couldn't believe it. No 'soft arse' and a clout. Was this another of Dave's sick jokes or was it really freedom?

'Thank you, nurse,' I said quickly, and walked past him into the passage.

'Right,' said Dave, moving his heavy body up some nearby stairs.

We turned at a landing and started up a second flight. I was well behind Dave, glad of the handrail to help this painful but hopeful journey.

Dave noticed I was well behind him. He turned and started down towards me. I felt certain that he was going to push me down the stairs.

'I can't take any more of you. Don't touch me!' I shouted

desperately.

Dave, to my complete surprise, helped me up the stairs, but, speaking close to my ear, warned me firmly, 'If you shout or say anything I don't like I'll break your bloody little arm clean off!'

At the top we soon came to the clearly-marked door of Dr C Wandless. I felt relieved that there seemed to be such a person. At this point, letting go of my arm, Dave whispered in my ear, 'Remember your girlfriend.' I gave him a bitterly angry but knowing glance, with my lips pressed tight together in temper.

Dr Wandless turned out to be definitely a lover of the colour brown. He was a man in his sixties who had perhaps decided to get closer to nature by making sure that all his clothes were a subtle mixture of varying shades of the same colour.

I was amazed, after Dave had been told he could go, that he said, 'Sir, I must just give Michael his watch back, which I have had in my pocket for safe keeping.'

The lying creep, I thought as I returned it to my wrist that had not noticed its absence.

Dr Wandless said I had been wrongly put in a padded cell owning to a small misunderstanding amongst the staff, the mistake being compounded by his colleague, Stuart Khan, being away on holiday. He said it was my wife Clare who discovered where I was and was able to alert the Hospital Director as to my whereabouts after she had tried to visit me earlier in the day.

I considered Dr Wandless's words carefully. I simply did not understand this man's casual attitude to my time in a padded cell. He did not seem to care, and he obviously had no idea about the extra treatment that his nurse, the loathsome Dave, enjoyed dosing out. At least he has a bowl of urine to clear up, I thought to myself smugly. Dr Wandless had also said that my wife Clare got me out of the cell. I remembered her so vaguely as the nice girl with the dark hair and oriental looks who I felt I had only met once. She had saved my life – probably quite literally. I would try to find a way to thank her as soon as I left this hospital.

Doctor Wandless continued, 'You looked vague when I

mentioned your wife, so I will read you some of your notes that have come across from "acute", in case you are unclear about anything else important.'

The doctor then played with his pipe, pressing his finger into the bowl before deciding to put the stem in his mouth and to apply a lit match over the compressed tobacco. After much sucking and exhaling, a wispy cloud of smoke hung in the air above his round face, with its well-trimmed beard and bespectacled eyes, before dispersing into the space of the room.

Satisfied that he was now ready and able to speak to me, he started to read out a few points which seemed to me to be chosen at random.

'You are twenty-six years old – just,' he pronounced, then looked up to see if I disagreed. 'Your mother died when you were six, and your father remarried and now lives in Canada. You were brought up by your grandmother in Basingstoke. You married Clare five years ago, and you have a son, David. Your present home is with your parents-in-law . . .'

I interrupted him and asked, although I couldn't picture her, 'Is my grandmother still alive?'

'No, I'm sorry, she died last year,' came a quiet, apologetic reply.

Leaning his pipe against the edge of a large hardwood ashtray partly filled with burnt tobacco, the doctor decided to continue the saga of my earlier life that remained blurred to me. 'Jobs, Michael,' he said, looking at me for a moment. 'You started to train as a solicitor's clerk, but hated it and dropped out. You have since tried several other jobs, including trainee laboratory technician and farm worker.'

Dr Wandless stopped talking, wondering to himself no doubt how much of what he had been telling me meant anything to me. He decided to make a cheerful comment. 'You are lucky, Michael, to have a nice-sounding wife like Clare to help you when your time comes to leave here.'

'Yes, I am,' I replied softly, while looking at the floor. My thoughts, however, were saying to me that I am even luckier to know and love Mary-Anne.

Dr Wandless was clearly restless. He kept packing and

repacking the charred remains in his pipe with his ash-covered forefinger, and at the same time he was fidgeting his body about in his chair as though it was impossible for him to get in a comfortable position. After what turned out to be a necessary part of his thought process, he said as though he was talking to his pipe, 'Michael, I think I can help you while your doctor is away. I want you to stay for a short time in the chronic men's section so that I can give you some more treatment which may help your memory and give your brain a beneficial rest.

2.

I could not believe how comfortable my new bedroom was after that damp cell. I had a really soft bed, a mirror to look at my bruises in, a wash basin and cupboards. It was a warm, cheerful-looking room, on the same floor as Dr Wandless's study. I had a limited view from the window of the steam coming out of the pipes in the kitchen roof and the tarmac road which circled the building, but that did not worry me. I just felt so relieved to be safe from the ravings of the pockmarked prison keeper, Dave.

A new nurse came to see me just as I was contemplating unpacking my pyjamas from my faithful small suitcase. He stood in front of me as I sat on the bed and held out his hand to offer me my evening medication. I observed that he was young, quite short, with curly brown hair. He had a chubby, flat face and a generous smile.

'My name is Peter,' he said gently, giving me a glass of water and watching me swallow the pills. 'Tomorrow you will go downstairs and eat with the other patients. In the evening there is a dance at 7.00 in the ladies' hall room. You might like to go to that. The next day, Monday, treatment starts, and you are to stay in your room.' Concluding my unexpected itinerary, Peter turned and started to leave, saying a mumbled, well-meant 'Good-night' as he left the room.

After a very welcome night's sleep in my quiet, comfortable room, I decided with some apprehension to go and join the other patients for some food.

I started to walk stiffly and with some discomfort as my bruised muscles objected to exercise. I began to climb carefully down some stairs near my room, which were new to me. As I listened, I could just hear a muted sound of people moving and talking down below.

On reaching the ground floor I found a large oak door half open with Peter standing beside it, clearly watching the activities on the other side. He turned to me and said, 'Come in, Michael, we are all one happy family in here.'

After passing several people whose faces looked disinterested by the presence of a 'new boy', Peter found me a place at a bench seat and some porridge in a tin bowl.

I looked around and tried to understand this strange place. The table was in the middle of a large room. There were men of all ages, shapes and sizes, sitting, lolling or even sleeping in different parts of the room. There was a man in one corner who particularly caught my attention, because he was completely naked. I was told later by Peter that he refused to get dressed, so they left him.

I noticed that quite a few patients were smoking, while one old boy hovered around waiting to pick up cigarette butts to smoke in his small brown pipe.

I started to spoon in some porridge, when a balding, dark-haired man sitting near me made it obvious he wanted my attention by saying, as a small boy might, 'Mister, mister, mister.' I turned to him. He immediately started to talk.

'When I was a child, someone shot an arrow through my head.' He then eagerly pointed with his finger to a dent and scarring on his forehead. Then, without pausing, he turned round to show me a second scar at the back of his head. 'This is where it came out,' he said. He looked back towards me, expecting some comment.

I felt like saying, 'Did you have an apple on your head at the time?' Instead I said what he wanted to hear. 'Well, that is quite remarkable. How do you feel now?'

'Better, thank you,' he said, looking pleased with himself and giving me a friendly, confused smile.

I had noticed that a number of the quietest men had a large scar down the middle of their foreheads. I had heard that by cutting certain nerve endings it was possible to affect the brain and thereby patients' behaviour. It seemed horrific to me as a way of helping people, but the men I could see looked content, but content children, not grown men.

I stopped gazing round the room for a moment and continued to eat. Bread, already buttered, followed the porridge. There was not a knife or breakable object in the room.

My eyes were soon drawn again to look at some of the inmates, for whom I felt so much empathy, more closely. Their eyes somehow indicated they were patients. Many carried a blank expression on their faces with a lost, helpless look in their eyes. There were no signs of frustration towards their 'prisoned' plight. I thought they were lovely people who indeed needed and deserved this protection from the hostile world outside.

I ate two meals with the chronically ill patients before retreating to my room. I lay on my soft bed and decided that I would give the dance at 7.00 a miss. My legs hurt, and anyway there was only one woman that I wanted to dance with. I expected and longed to be with her quite soon. Then I wondered how Mary-Anne was coping in her room in the other building only a hundred yards away. Was she missing me, I asked myself? I certainly missed her beauty, her strength of character and, of course, her cheerful, chuckling, smiling face. I pursued the fanciful hope in my daydreaming thoughts that she would walk through my door now and just look at me with those laughing eyes. My life would begin again.

3.

On Monday morning I did not have time to get out of bed before receiving an early visit from Dr Wandless and Peter. With the bowl of his meerschaum pipe held in the palm of one hand and brushing a little surplus ash off his brown corduroy jacket with the other, Dr Wandless said, 'Right, Michael,' looking straight at my half awake eyes, 'I am going to send you to sleep for today. Peter will give you some tablets and a glass of milk. I will come and see you tomorrow.'

As I lay in bed with a belly full of milk and sleeping pills, and having suffered the indignity of a mouth check, I asked myself in the brief moment before sleep overcame me: what are they doing to me now?

I awoke to find the room was slightly dark. I felt bilious and giddy. I eventually found the basin and regurgitated the little in my stomach. Peter must have heard me, and appeared in my room as if from nowhere.

'Michael, you're awake early,' he said brightly. 'It's only five-thirty in the morning. Go next door to the toilet if you need to, and then lie on your bed. The doctor will be in soon.' As he turned and left he said, with feeling, 'Don't worry about the basin.'

'Don't worry about the basin,' I repeated to myself crossly. Blast the basin! What about how dreadful I was feeling?

Dr Wandless arrived bright and cheerful, in total contrast to my mind. 'I'm going to increase your dose of pills today. You are not staying asleep for long enough,' he announced in an unquestionable manner. I was not given leave for even a humble appeal as the milk, pills and mouth check followed immediately.

Over a period of four days and nights this strange routine continued. I felt worse, which I considered was barely possible, every time I woke. Each day the pill dose was increased because I apparently did not sleep for long enough to satisfy my doctor.

On the fourth occasion that I woke from my enforced soporific state, the discomfort from my head and stomach was desperately intense. I knew that I had definitely and absolutely had enough of this obscure daily 'hibernation' therapy, induced by a seemingly random use of narcotics.

Right on cue, after my visit to the basin, Dr Wandless and Peter arrived. Dr Wandless was still colour-consciously dressed, looking like a well-dug soil sample. He appeared to be in excellent health, which was more than could be said about his patient.

'Good morning, Michael, it's eight o'clock,' he said chirpily, followed by, 'You do wake early! I wanted you to sleep till nearer noon. What shall we do with him, nurse?'

he said, looking out of the window at nothing in particular. Peter knew not to reply, and stood with an air of ignorance about him, near the door.

Dr Wandless made me get out of bed before peering closely at the state of my tired eyes. Satisfied by his very limited examination of me, he said with confidence, 'We will give it one more crack.'

No you damn well won't! I said categorically to myself.

'We will up the dose,' he continued, fortunately unable to perceive my thoughts.

After some words on his way out with Peter, Dr Wandless left the room mumbling, with his back to me, 'See you tomorrow, Michael.' I thought, that is most unlikely, if I can possibly avoid it.

Peter gave me a glass of milk, then handed me my pills and watched me swallow them. Still not completely convinced, he checked the hidden corners of my mouth with three practiced fingers of his right hand. I got back into bed and tried to look settled and almost asleep. To give him extra encouragement to leave me quickly I said, in a gentle, drowsy voice, 'Thank you, Peter, see you on Saturday.'

He took the hint and turned and started to walk away before saying, 'Sleep as long as possible,' as he closed the door behind him.

I immediately tossed back the covers, got to the sink, shoved two fingers to the back of my throat and brought up my pills. I was pleased to see them slide down the side of the sink.

My sheer determination to escape this vile treatment and this whole crazy building enabled me partially to forget the discomfort and droopiness my body was suffering.

I changed into my few clothes and packed my pyjamas into my small case where they joined my birthday card and wash bag. I knew that I was not able to run very fast, so I decided to stroll confidently out as though I owned the place.

Before I knew it, I was out in the sunshine, walking towards the main gate. I may have looked confident, but in reality I was absolutely terrified. My heart was pumping fast, my knees were shaky and my narcotic-affected vision was blurred. However, as though by some kind of miracle, I kept moving and was not recognized.

At the edge of the road beyond the gates panic set in as I realized that I had entered the outside world that did not know me. I saw a gap in the traffic but couldn't judge the speed of the oncoming car. There was a screech of brakes as the driver reacted to my ill-timed moment to cross the road. I was soon walking slowly past the dress shop. I thought briefly of the red ballgown, but kept walking.

I was soon on the pavement of the high street, trembling with fear and indecision. I felt pleased to have escaped, but concerned that I had no idea where I was trying to escape to.

I noticed the cake shop was open behind me. As I started to turn round so that I could look carefully at the window, I heard a voice from a loudhailer and then saw a police car moving slowly along the road.

'We are looking for twenty-six-year-old Michael Simpson. He has dark brown hair and is . . .' The car with the microphone had gone past me and the police message faded into the distance. Why are they looking for me, I wondered with horror? I was not a criminal. I had not hurt anyone. They should not be after me, but that brutal nurse Dave should be locked up, and soon.

I was shocked to find that I was 'on the run', particularly as I hadn't realized that the hospital would put the police onto me. I looked both ways along the pavement to see if there was a policeman in sight or if anyone appeared to be looking closely at me. I seemed safe for the moment and decided to risk going into the cake shop. Once inside, I knew that the staff could not have heard the police announcement.

Two gingerbread men, please,' I said boldly, having decided that I could not cope with the cream cakes on offer. I noticed I had just twenty-five pounds and a crumpled chequebook as I returned my money with the change to my pocket.

On leaving the shop I went and lent against a nearby telephone kiosk and bit the legs off my biscuits. Soon they were gone, and the problem of what to do next loomed larger than before. I thought about money for food and a room somewhere. I had the idea that my chequebook would be dangerous to use. There may not be any money in the bank account and I would be asked for some form of identification, which I hadn't got and didn't want. At that moment I wished I could change my height and dye my hair pink!

Who in this town of Nimbrington would help me, I asked myself as I slouched against the kiosk's red-framed windows? I could not think of anyone, and then I was inspired at last by the sight of the telephone receiver. I thought of Clare. I straight away fought with the strongly sprung door in order to get myself and my case inside.

I found the Drillingham number which she had written on my birthday card. I dialled 100 and asked to reverse the charges and prayed that I wasn't speaking to Dawn. It would have been a complication that I did not need at that moment.

There was a very obvious tremor in my hand as I held onto the phone and waited for Clare to answer. The notice on the side of the box was unreadable to me. It might have said, for all I could tell, 'Dogs and suitcases are not allowed in this box. Sitting or praying are absolutely prohibited.'

I heard Clare answer. 'Hullo Michael, I guessed it was you. Are you ringing from the hospital?'

'No, I've run away. Can you help me?' I said loudly down the bad line.

I could just decipher her voice amongst the crackling noises. 'But you haven't been discharged, and it's a six hour round trip to West Nimbrington from Drillingham.'

'Where is Drillingham?' I asked, although not knowing where my wife lived sounded unlikely to be of any immediate concern. She must have moved, I thought, feeling annoyed at the inconvenience it was causing me.

'It's in Norfolk. You can come here, darling,' she said feebly, 'when the doctors say you are well enough. Now be a good chap and go back to the hospital. Bye, darling, I'll come and visit you next month.'

Just the dialling tone was left buzzing in my ear.

Back on the pavement, clutching my case, I felt thrown into further confusion. I had expected Clare, who I thought was so nice and kind, to help me. What was I to do now? I knew I had to sit down, and badly needed a drink of anything. I'd even be pleased with a glass of milk.

I decided to wander down a side street, hoping for the unexpected to come to my aid. I felt mentally so confused and physically so frail that I quite expected to pass out at any time. I was certain that I must have absorbed some of those pills. I had no choice but to dump my tired and trembling body on the pavement and to lean back against a convenient garden wall.

I closed my eyes and tried to clarify my strange situation. I dare not go back to the hospital while more narcotics or a cell were a possibility, although I would go if I was certain that I could have my old room back in the Acute building and be able to see Mary-Anne. I now saw that I could not take refuge with my wife because she assumed all doctors knew best and seemed to consider she was living in another country. I was also quite frightened of the West Nimbrington world that I had walked into.

I was gradually feeling that I was not alone. I slowly opened my eyes, gazed lethargically and with no purpose into the daylight, until I saw a thin pair of women's legs quite close to me. I looked up and saw a pale face and a mass of blonde hair looking over me. A gentle but feeble voice said, 'It's Jill. You bought me a drink once in "The George", remember? You look sick, and you can't stay here.'

'My name is Michael. Jill, please help me,' I implored her as I raised a hand towards her.

Jill helped me to my feet. I stood for a moment with my arm round her shoulders while she told me, 'I've got a room in a house up the road. My landlady's gone shopping. I could sneak you in and you could have a rest till you feel better.'

I thought it was kind of her, but felt it was unlikely I would ever actually feel better. 'Thank you, Jill,' I said gratefully as I held onto her for the hundred yard walk to the door of a Victorian terraced house. She quickly unlocked the door and helped me climb the stairs to her tiny, chaotic bedroom.

I lay on the unmade single bed while she started to tidy

the jumble of clothes strewn across the floor. 'I usually do this later,' she said, untwisting a small bra.

I noticed blue pills beside the bed. 'Jill, you don't take these, do you?' I enquired, holding one up for her to see.

'No, I don't,' she said firmly. 'I just sell them.'

While Jill quietly tidied up, I tried in vain to relax. I dozed a little, but was unable to fall asleep. Later, Jill asked me why I was in this state. She seemed to understand all she wanted to know. She was sympathetic but not caringly loving.

As the light through the windows began to fade a little, Jill looked at her watch and said, 'I must get ready to go out.'

'Where are you going?' I said, still lying flat on my back on her bed.

'Where I always go to work. Round the pubs and clubs, of course.'

'Do you bring men back here?' I said, considering my own position.

'If I'm lucky,' she said, with a coy smile.

'How much do you usually make in one evening?'

'About twenty quid,' she said, unzipping the back of her daytime dress.

'Jill, I've got nowhere to go tonight. May I stay here? I can give you twenty pounds,' I said, staring with vagueness at her slim, trim body, clothed only in petite underwear. Compared with Mary-Anne, she seemed to me to have the features of little more than a fragile child.

She swivelled round on her make-up stool and said in her practised manner, 'Do you want to sleep with me, then?' As though I was selecting from a menu.

I replied, 'Just half the bed for one night, and I don't feel up to sex, but a cuddle to help calm me down would be nice.'

'All right,' she said, purposefully approaching the bed, 'give me the twenty quid and you can stay till the morning.' I handed the money over, feeling thankful, while I continued to lie fully-dressed on the whole bed.

Jill then declared, 'Food is a problem if you are not well enough to go somewhere. The landlady makes all her lodgers eat the food they cook in the kitchen, and guests

84

are not permitted. How about a cheese and pickle sandwich? I bought them yesterday.'

Pickle was not a soothing thought for my stomach, but as there was no alternative food on offer, I accepted. 'Thank you, Jill. Let's eat them now.'

We did and Jill drank half a bottle of doubtful-looking red wine left by a 'friend' the night before. I stayed with several glasses of lukewarm tap water.

'It's nice not having to dress again,' said Jill, smiling at me while her small, neat figure perched on the edge of the bed.

After an hour or so of slow chat we had the curtains pulled and a bedside light with a dim, red glow switched on.

'What's in that funny little brown case?' she said inquisitively.

'Pyjamas,' I replied.

'Forget about them,' she said in a small but commanding voice, moving my case further away from the bed with her foot.

As Jill stood up and removed her bra and pants, all the indications were that it was bedtime. After a struggle, and with Jill's help, all my clothes had joined the jumble on the floor. As we both got under the bed covers, I wondered why I ever thought there was room for both in this bed, except, of course, in a stacked position.

I cuddled Jill a little. She was soft but small and bony. At one point I held her tight and just sobbed into her pile of unkempt blonde hair. This upset her so she rolled over to one edge of the bed and let the wine and her financial success take her to her dreams.

I lay awake for most of the night, unable to move for fear of waking Jill. It occurred to me that Jill could probably make love in her sleep and might turn over at any moment in a sex-demanding dream phase.

I could not relax, and thought anxiously about my problems that were really robbing me of my sleep and which, unlike Jill, would not go away. My concern was for my predicament and tomorrow's unplanned day.

In the morning when Jill's 'in-built clock' demanded, she suddenly climbed over me, switched off the red 'I like to see what I'm doing' light and said sleepily, 'Morning, Michael, sleep OK?' as she left the bed. She pulled the curtains and announced it was a lovely day before I could reply.

In spite of having a full and private view of a small, naked female, I felt absolutely terrible. I was shaking with nervousness, combined with tiredness and sickness. At that moment I wished I was a healthy and content prostitute. At least I would know where this disorientated mind and body of mine belonged in this confusing life.

'Jill, I decided last night what I'm going to do,' I said, watching her find her clothes from the floor in the wrong order.

'Yes,' she said, 'tell me,' as she clipped together the back of her bra and looked at the carpet.

'I'm going to go back to the hospital and my old room,' I said, expecting some reaction. Her mind was evidently elsewhere.

I dressed with difficulty, gave Jill a kiss and thanked her. Then, when Jill said the landlady was out of sight, I made my way into the streets of Nimbrington.

As I started to walk a route to the hospital, my body was in much discomfort. I thought about the relative safety of my old hospital room that I had mentioned as a reason to Jill for me to go back. It certainly was not the deciding factor. That was Mary-Anne. I needed to be with her and her laughter, vitality and strength. I walked a little faster at the thought of seeing her.

Inside the hospital grounds I kept well wide of the 'chronic section', hoping that Dr Wandless couldn't see for pipe smoke, or perhaps was asleep himself.

I was met by Graham as I struggled through the main entrance. 'Well, you are back, Michael,' he said with a smile, while stating the obvious. 'Wait in the treatment room. I will get the doctor.'

Dr Khan examined me and commented to the nurse that he had seen fighter pilots after a crash in less of a state of nervous shock than I was in. 'You may go back to your old room, Michael, but stay in bed today. Graham will look after you,' he instructed, in what I thought was one of his more understanding moods, for which I was grateful.

86

Back in my old bed I began to relax. I thought of the pleasure and joy to come tomorrow when I would be with Mary-Anne. She was indeed the only person that made my life worth living.

7

1.

I woke up in the middle of the night, screaming and gasping for air. My eyes opened into total darkness as I shook momentarily with fright. I breathed heavily with relief as I realized that the pock-marked fiend was not about to put the boot into my still bruised body.

A calmer sleep returned as I warmed still more to the sanctuary of my own friendly familiar room.

I woke to the sound of Doris dropping in the paper, followed by her comment, 'If you sleep much nearer the edge of the bed you'll fall out!' As she bustled on her way, I knew that my subconscious had made me allow space for Jill's slim naked body.

I lay my head back into the middle of the pillow where it belonged, and felt relaxed about the day to come for the first time since I was taken away.

I let my mind enjoy pleasant thoughts. I would soon see Mary-Anne and tell her of my adventures. She would laugh and giggle. She was certain to make light of all my traumatic moments which would help me to remember that with her I was in my earthly paradise, where the world was no longer hostile, provided, like her, you didn't take it too seriously.

'Are you having breakfast today?' enquired a familiar voice through a half-open door.

'Graham, you startled me. I was thinking about more important matters than breakfast,' I replied, quite surprised to be jolted out of my meditation.

'Look,' Graham said, 'you have your own television set.' He pointed at an unsightly glass-fronted grey box.

'I don't want a television,' I insisted as I sat up in bed

to glare at the thing with disapproval. 'It's worse than the newspapers,' I said, getting up and going through my shredding routine with my unread newsprint. Then I looked straight at Graham and explained. 'I don't want to know about media fiction or exaggerated angled truths. The whole of my life seems like one big stage play to me as it is, but the ruddy producer has never found me a part. I'm just a member of a bored, disgruntled audience.'

At this point I felt Graham had fallen into this category; he was standing by the television with his mouth half-open, looking at me as if I was strongly abnormal. 'There is some good sport on this evening,' he said leaving the room, not understanding a word I had said.

I was soon dressed, perfectly clean-shaven, with my hair combed neatly to the shape of my head. I hoped Mary-Anne would not worry about my clothes, because they were the same tatty collection that I had lived in for a long time. 'Now to find that lovely lady,' I said aloud, as I slipped into the passage.

I passed Sam. I thought he must have changed, but no. 'Got a gun, Michael?' he asked as I walked by.

'Sorry, mate,' I replied.

Near the start of the ladies' section, I noticed Sylvia leaning casually against the wall as though she was waiting for a 'pick-up'. She looked more outsize than ever, poor thing. I went up to her, which encouraged her to give me a chubby smile. 'Hi Michael,' she said, running a hand over some of her more explosive contours.

'Sylvia,' I said earnestly, 'is now a good time to see Mary-Anne? Are there any staff nurses on the prowl?' She looked at me with a smile in her eyes and put a hand over her mouth while she laughed and rocked her flab. It was as though I was a fool to ask such a question.

'Why are you laughing, Sylvia?' I cried. 'I must see Mary-Anne!'

Looking more serious she said gently, but with no sign of regret, 'Mary-Anne left last week. Why don't you take me out instead?'

I didn't reply, but ran upstairs to Mary-Anne's room. I discovered to my horror that it was not just empty, but quite unlived in. I ran down and into the female nurses' room. 'What are you doing in here?' said a senior nurse indignantly.

'I'm looking for Mary-Anne,' I said desperately.

'Miss Mary-Anne Cheyney was discharged last Monday, and returned to London,' said a pompous staff nurse's voice.

'Where in London?' I shouted.

'You aren't going anywhere, so there is no need for you to know. Go back to the men's area,' the pompous voice replied angrily.

I ran out to the corridor and back towards Henry's room. I hoped frantically that he had not also been discharged. I was in a terrible state of panic. I needed a friend to talk to. Everything I'd hoped and planned for seemed to have gone wrong.

'Thank God you're in, Henry!' I said as I rushed into his room. Not waiting to catch my breath, I exclaimed, 'Mary-Anne has gone, and I'm stuck here! What the hell am I going to do?'

'Calm down,' said Henry, 'sit on the bed and let's talk about it. It's nice to see you back, or perhaps I shouldn't say that now,' he said, biting his tongue. 'By the way, you are stuck here for the moment. Graham told me this morning that the nurses are keeping a careful watch on you, so you can't run away again. Graham even had the cheek to ask me to watch out for you!'

'Blast Graham! Blast all the nurses!' I said crossly. 'How, Henry, am I going to get discharged so that I can be with Mary-Anne in London? This time I get out, I don't want the police looking for me,' I said emphatically.

Henry leant forward on the edge of his bed and clasped his hands together in deep thought. He broke the brief silence by saying gently, 'Do you really feel well enough to travel to London and live there?'

'If it means being with Mary-Anne, yes!' I said quickly.

'Where does she live?' asked Henry.

'In her father's flat,' I replied vaguely. 'It's somewhere in a place called Eaton Square.'

'She has no mother?'

'I don't think so, she never mentioned her. Henry,' I confessed, 'I do not have a phone number of the flat or a full address. It could be any one of hundreds in the Square for all I know.'

'Look,' said Henry, 'there is a female nurse who likes me. I might be able to get her to find out the address from the records. Now you ring the doctor who sent you here and ask for help to get you out. Tell him you are feeling well enough to go home.'

'I don't know the number and I can't even remember his name. Anyway, home is meant to be in Norfolk, not London. I will ring another person I know,' I said. I thought, as Henry was helping me to find Mary-Anne, it would be wrong to confuse him by telling him about Clare's existence.

I set off from Henry's room straightaway, prepared to ring my wife, something not popular the last time I tried it. I used the nurses' phone and got through quickly. I said imploringly, 'You must help to get me discharged, darling, or I may stay here for years. They can forget about people in here.' I decided that I daren't tell her that I wanted to be in London, but I felt if she could get me discharged I would use her car to get to London.

Clare's faint voice sounded unconvincing. 'I will try, but I'll have to do what the doctors say is best for you.'

Her words echoed in my ears. My hopes for an early release were not high. I wandered into the garden and noticed a nurse was following me. When I came to the beech tree I stopped and looked at the soft green grass where Mary-Anne used to lie. I pretended I could see her gorgeous sensual body smiling at me. 'Why did you have to leave? Why, my love, no message or phone number? When will I next see you? I need you, Mary-Anne, all of you,' I said out loud; my impassioned words seemed to disperse round the trunk of the tree.

My nursing watchdog kindly kept his distance. He must have known that I needed time and space to clear my jumbled thoughts. Indeed, I felt very delicate. Just a slight picture in my mind of Mary-Anne was enough to make me weep helplessly, as though she was lost for ever.

2.

After a month of dwindling hope, spent dragging my bored, miserable self-pitying body from place to place, I received some dramatic news from Clare.

Large black handwriting on blue notepaper told me that in one week's time I was to be transferred from St Matthews to a small psychiatric unit called the Duke Clinic at St Lukes, a large London hospital. Clare said she would drive me there. I could not believe my luck. I was going to London! I might be allowed out to look for Eaton Square. Then I could knock on all the doors until I found my Mary-Anne!

I rushed round to Henry's room and told him about my letter.

'I'm delighted,' he said, 'I think I'll be out soon, too. I'm afraid that I have not been able to get that address you wanted. The nurse I was going to talk to always appears to be off sick.'

'Don't worry, Henry. Thank you for trying,' I said. 'I'll find it when I get to London.'

I imagined that everyone must have noticed a change for the better in my appearance and behaviour during those last seven days. Even Dr Khan said obligingly, 'You are walking better, Michael.' He also said, 'You have a very determined wife. If it wasn't for her, we would not be letting you go yet.'

On the due date for my departure I felt very cheerful and excited. There was no worry or feeling of appre-hension towards going to the Duke Clinic for the first time. The thought foremost in my mind was that I was going to London!

Waiting eagerly at the door with my small suitcase and Graham by my side, I saw a large dark blue Wolseley pull up by the door, with Clare's dark head of hair almost hidden behind the steering wheel.

'That's a 6/99,' volunteered Graham. I was impressed. I'd never considered before that Graham might know anything about anything outside this hospital.

I waved to Henry as he stood by his bedroom door, looking sad.

'Good luck, my friend. You next,' I called out. Then I shook hands with Graham, who meant well even though he did not speak. I remembered that he was not given to releasing charm on such occasions.

Clare leaned over and opened the passenger door for me from the inside of the car.

'Sorry we are in a hurry,' she called to Graham. 'Jump in, Michael. Your case can go on the floor,' she directed in a confident voice. I noticed she was wearing a smart blue suit that only slightly clashed with the colour of the car. Her face was well made-up, with her narrow black eyebrows an attractive feature, but as I got into the car I was wondering if they were hair or paint.

We drove off for London at a graceful speed. After several miles, I tried to get orientated to the world outside the hospital. It seemed to me that every car and pedestrian that I saw was moving unusually fast, with a strange unknown purpose pursuing them to their destination.

I looked at the side of Clare's face and decided to try and soften her determined, concentrating driver's expression.

'Clare,' I said gently, 'thank you for getting me a place at the Duke Clinic in London. How did you manage it?'

'I pulled a lot of strings,' she said. 'After a lot of hard work, trying to convince him you would be better off in his hands, Dr Chipotski agreed to take you. The clinic is small. I think you will like it,' she said, without being able to take her eyes off the road.

After a few moments' silence I asked, 'Clare, why do you live in Drillingham. I've never heard of the place.'

Clare seemed surprised by the question and said, 'I thought you knew that Daddy bought it for us six months ago so that we could move out of his Basingstoke house and be independent. He knew I loved Norfolk and wanted more space for my dogs. By the way, we were also told by Daddy's doctor that if we bought a small farm, as you get better, it might be good for you to put your year's farm training into practice.' She shook her head slightly and said, 'I'm sure I told you all about it months ago, your memory never was very good at the best of times.'

'How much land is there?' I asked with some trepidation, remembering how wealthy her father was.

'Two hundred acres,' she said without hesitating, 'and I keep twenty acres of rough grass for my dogs to run in.'

For heaven's sake, what dogs and how many that need twenty acres, I thought! I dare not ask her at the moment. She would be even ruder about my memory.

Clare continued. 'It is called Willowpit Farm. You will love it. We have two men at the moment who you can help when you are well enough.'

'Does the farm make enough money for us?' I asked.

'Well, not really,' she confessed, 'it's more of a "hobby farm". It's a long-term investment for Daddy, which helps my dogs and will give you some occupational therapy. Daddy, the sweet man, still gives me an allowance. Oh! He bought this car, do you like it?' I looked at the leather seats, the walnut fascia and my pretty, well-dressed wife. I thought they all went well together, and managed with no enthusiasm to emit a quiet, 'Yes, I like dark blue.'

I had expected Clare to have mentioned our four-year-old son by now.

'Darling,' I said with affection. I paused as the sound of my voice seemed to hang in the air. I felt that my manner of speaking was false, and 'darling' should only be said with loving emotion to my first love in London. I repeated myself, but in a matter-of-fact tone that was better suited to our relationship, which seemed brief and untried.

'Darling, where is David today?'

'Oh, don't worry about him,' she said assuredly. 'He is playing with our neighbour, Jake Paddington. He often takes David round his farm in his Land Rover. David loves it. Jake has no children, and adopts David for the day whenever it's going to help me.' There was a temporary stop in her chatter. It gave me a moment to feel some disappointment that my son, who I hardly remembered, seemed to have been given an alternative father figure in my absence.

'You will like Jake,' Clare continued in her instructing voice. 'He swam freestyle for the British team a few years ago, and he has his own enormous swimming pool.'

I plunged in with the final important question. 'Does this Jake chap live on his own?'

'No,' said Carol clearly. 'He has his own elderly

housekeeper, who is usually drunk.'

My vision of Jake was getting less bearable by the minute. I could picture a musclebound, monied man, who was probably a devious opportunist.

We started to hit heavier traffic, so I guessed that we were moving into the big city. I considered it strange that Clare had not once asked me how I felt. I sometimes thought that she could be so embarrassed by my answers that she preferred not to know. I remember now that once I told her that I could not cope with life anymore. She promptly got in the car and drove to a friend's house, where she stayed for a week. I decided to play it her way and not speak about my unmentionable problems.

I recognized Nelson's Column as we made slow bumper to bumper progress, and I wondered if cars had been a sensible invention. At yet another set of traffic lights Clare said, 'We are nearly there. St Lukes, I'm told, is a tall building round the corner on the left. Keep an eye out. It should have a small car park in front of it.'

We arrived thanks to a large helpful sign. Armed with a small suitcase and a lady that I felt I hardly knew, I approached the main door, intent on finding a lift to take us to the fourth floor.

3.

A male nurse showed us to my room, which had windows allowing a partial view of the road below. The nurse was a big man. Perhaps there was a height requirement in order to be a psychiatric nurse, as in the police force, I thought.

'Put you pyjamas on, and stay in bed until I tell you to get up,' said the nurse firmly. His words reminded me of the poor lady who was told the same thing by her doctor and spent thirty years in bed unnecessarily, before another doctor discovered her and countermanded the instruction. I decided one day would be quite enough for me.

My room was very comfortable, and I was particularly delighted that I would be able to look for Mary-Anne out

95

of the window amongst the people walking by.

Clare, on the other hand, was looking out of the window at the sky. I wondered what held her gaze and why she seemed to be in deep thought about somewhere miles from this clinic.

I bounced in my pyjamas on the bed and said to Clare, 'I will soon be out of here.'

Clare smiled, gave me a peck on the cheek and left, saying, 'Wait and see. I will ring you.'

The very pale, tall dark-haired nurse, whose name I had discovered was Tim, gave me a sheet of paper and a pen as I lay in bed. He said, 'Please fill this in for us, I will be back in fifteen minutes to collect it.'

Having quickly read the first question, I called to Tim as he was leaving, 'Tim, what does this mean, "would you rather be a wrestler or a boxer?" I don't want to be either.'

Tim looked back at me and replied as though my question was foolish. 'You have to tick one of the two alternatives. We will learn a great deal about your personality from the results.'

Tim left the room. I saw no sense in any of the questions, so I ticked the options at random. Tim soon took the form away, looking at me as he did so as if to say, 'Good, you've toed the line so far'.

The next day, after a pleasantly surprising cereal and boiled egg breakfast, Tim told me to get up and get ready to see Dr Chipotski in his room nearly opposite mine.

Dr Chipotski's green leather, gold-tooled desktop had nothing on it at all, not even a speck of dust, I suspected. I watched the great doctor from my small armchair in front of him. He appeared to be in his sixties, with white hair and a kind wrinkled lived-in face.

He looked at me like a benevolent uncle and said in a soft deep voice, 'From your appearance and what we have been told about you, Michael, you are clearly a nice chap.' I smiled warmly at the compliment. 'This is one of your problems,' he said, to my complete surprise.

He continued, '"Nice chaps" often end up keeping everyone around them happy, and then often find themselves unhappy and isolated. Do you understand the point I am making?' he asked, looking at me carefully.

'Yes, you are right,. I don't like upsetting people if I can possibly avoid it, and I usually lean over backwards to avoid any chance of bad feeling,' I said honestly, having never thought about this subject before. It did occur to me that perhaps this discussion was as a direct result of the questionnaire that I had shown little respect for.

Dr Chipotski then said in his positive manner, 'It's a small point, but it may help you to think about it.'

He leant back in his chair, glanced at his bare desk and then said, 'Now, I will be making some medication changes, which I think will help to reduce the number of occasions that you find yourself in a very depressed mood.' I immediately insisted to myself in my mind that there was only one medication which worked for me and that was being with my tall, cheerful, curly-headed Mary-Anne. I always felt well and at my best in her company.

The doctor said, cutting short my daydreaming, 'I will be seeing you again soon. Don't leave the unit. You had better go now and join the other patients for lunch.'

Lunch was eaten round a small pine table. To my surprise there were only ten of us, and all but me were teenage girls. All the girls bar one were painfully thin, and I recognized them as being anorexic. The one pretty chubby one was dark-haired. She called herself Sue, but worried me because she had an obvious round blistered burn mark on her cheek.

A cheerful sister, dressed in navy blue with a delicately folded doily-like hat pinned cleverly to her hair, put a plate full of appetizing food in front of each of us.

Sue and I started to eat and enjoy our meal; when sister had left us, the other girls scraped part of their food on to one plate. They then stacked all the plates in the middle of the table with some uneaten food pressed between them.

As I continued to eat, with some embarrassment, I realized that now the 'owner' of any one particular girl's plate could not be identified. Sister returned and understood what had happened, and perhaps deciding she should not have left the room, cleared up and said nothing. She did, however, look annoyed.

At this point everyone left the room, leaving sister with

no chance to serve a pudding if she had one. I strolled across the landing to my room and sat in my small well-sprung armchair that faced the window. I used the end of the bed as a footrest and tried to relax. I decided to let my mind wander over my first morning at the Duke Clinic. It seemed clear to me that it was a civilized homely place, but I was already missing not being able to walk outside, round the path to the beech tree and across the soft green grass of the golf course.

Dr Chipotski seemed a kind man, I reflected, although I was sure he wouldn't understand that for me to be with Mary-Anne was what I needed and not more and more strange pills. When he mentioned new medication, he was probably referring to some new mind-blowing anti-depressant that even made you feel happy in a padded cell. I said to myself firmly that I did not want my moods to be controlled by chemical concoctions being introduced to my body. I suspected, however, that I would have to try them.

I thought back to lunchtime. I felt very sorry for those thin, wasted young girls, and wished that I knew how to help them. I did not know the reason for some girls, particularly in their teens, refusing to eat. I remembered that I was told by one doctor that if a lady became thin enough, her periods would stop. He said that maybe this was how some of our thinner saints never had children, had no sexual desire and were able to remain virgins for life with little effort! However, the young girls in this hospital were hardly trying to be beatified. They desperately needed effective help before it was too late. I couldn't believe from their facial expressions at lunchtime that they wanted to die.

I knew that Sue with a sore face was a very different case. I hoped that she was somebody who would enjoy talking to me.

The door was unexpectedly opened by Tim, and in doing so he dislodged my legs from their 'at rest' position.

'Michael,' he said, handing me a small grey book and a pencil, 'this is an IQ test that we would like you to do. If you look at the first page, you will see that it is self-explanatory. I will collect the book in exactly twenty minutes.'

'If I'm proved stupid will I be given the appropriate brain-boosting tablets?' I asked sarcastically.

'Just get on with it. You have nineteen minutes left,' Tim said as he walked out of my room.

As I waded through the book, it seemed to me like a catalogue of various designs of Persian rugs. The only thing they had in common was that they all had small holes in them and I had to find the correct missing patterned piece to fill the holes from the selection provided.

I finished the book before Tim returned and collected it. I had to admit to myself that I did not understand the point of the test. It seemed to have little to do with IQ and I didn't want to acquire skills as a Persian rug patcher.

I stood up by the window for much of that afternoon and looked intently at the people walking on the pavement on the far side of the road. Indeed, over the weeks to come I was to spend more time looking and hoping, against anything my commonsense told me, for Mary-Anne.

I could see so many people wearing big coats and headscarves, and most of them walked very fast, as though they were trying to cross hot coals in bare feet.

I didn't think Mary-Anne would ever conform or be traditional. She would leave her curly blonde hair blowing in the wind. I was sure that I would spot her one day and then zoom down in the lift and grab her.

I felt certain that she must go out for a walk occasionally, and there was a chance Eaton Square was not far away. Stupidly, I was worried about asking in case I was told it was not within walking distance. I believe, while I remained ignorant, there was some hope. I also knew that there was a chance that Mary-Anne had found out where I was, after a possible tittering phone call to St Matthews.

Later that evening, having gained sister's permission, I walked along the carpeted landing to arrive at Sue's room. I called at the door, 'Sue, it's Michael, the new patient. May I come in?'

'Yes, of course,' came the sound of a cheerful young female voice.

Sue was sitting up in bed with a book on her lap. The room was gently lit and very welcoming. Sue, wearing a pretty pink nightie, was looking calm and comfortable. As I sat down in her armchair, I noticed once more the circular red sore on the side of her face.

'Have you been in this clinic for long?' I enquired.

'Just four weeks. I came in on my seventeenth birthday, but I was pleased. I like it here,' she said, flicking, with a shake of her head, some of her straight dark hair so that by accident or design it partially covered her wound.

'You are not like the other thin girls. In fact, you and I are the odd ones out,' I said, trying to indicate we had something in common. 'Sue, tell me why you are in here,' I asked kindly.

There was no hesitation from Sue; she seemed pleased to talk and said, 'I keep hurting myself, and my father sent me in here to try and get them to stop me doing it.'

'You mean like your cheek,' I suggested.

'Yes,' she said, 'a cigarette burn. I've got seven altogether. Let me show you,' she said with surprising keenness. She straightaway pulled back the bedcovers and revealed her young legs beneath her nightie.

'Come and have a look,' she requested. I hesitated in my chair for a moment, then I decided to do what she wanted, and so I went and stood by her bedside. She took me on a tour of her body, pointing with the forefinger of her right hand, and counting out loud at the same time. I looked with horror at seven large inflamed round blistered burns. They were mainly on her thighs and her arms. I thought it so sad that a young attractive girl should find it necessary to scar her body for life.

'Why do you do this to yourself, Sue?' I asked.

'I'm not sure,' she said, looking concerned, 'but the way my father treats me doesn't help.'

'I noticed that one of your burns has nearly healed. Will you let them all get better? They will leave a permanent scar but they will feel more comfortable,' I said, wondering if I could help her.

'I know', she said, pulling the covers back over her damaged legs. 'When one heals, I light up a cigarette and make another burn mark!' she added, to my astonishment.

I looked at her young blemished face and said, 'Sue, I don't know what to say to you. I don't know enough about this kind of thing, but it seems to me a crying shame that you freely damage forever your attractive young body. Would it help if I took your cigarettes away?' I said, feeling totally inadequate.

'No, Michael, I can get some more, and just one cigarette can be used several times.'

I realized now that, out of inquisitiveness, I had barged into Sue's personal problems and then found that they were more than I could understand or cope with. 'Sue,' I asked, 'is Dr Chipotski helping you?'

'He tries hard and is kind, but as yet he and I cannot seem to get to the heart of the matter. I think the doctor is going to talk to my father soon,' she said sombrely, as though such talks could be productive.

I held her hand, leant forward and said softly, 'Take care of yourself, you are more precious than you seem to realize. I will see you at breakfast.'

Back in my room, I lay in bed thinking with regret about my limitations, before allowing sleep to start and shut my mind. I knew of no way that I could help the desperately thin girls, and now the remaining patient, Sue, seemed beyond my pathetic desires to help. As my eyes closed I asked myself, why could life be so cruel to people's minds, causing them to want to severely harm themselves, when in fact they wanted to go on living?

In the morning, Tim brought in a copy of *The Times* newspaper and left it on my bed. On this occasion I had no desire to tear it up. Instead I thumbed through the paper, looking at the pictures and the headlines.

To my amazement, on page twelve I saw a photograph of an elderly man that I thought I knew. He had a balding head, an intelligent face and piercing eyes that seemed to be watching me.

I started to read what was written under the picture, and was shocked. It said, 'Sir Robert Cheyney, a captain of industry for forty years, died today aged sixty-nine. Sir Robert leaves one daughter.' Then it recorded his gallant war record and his chairmanship for fifteen years of this country's largest public brewery chain. He also apparently had worked as an economic advisor to the government.

How dreadful, I thought. Poor Mary-Anne had lost her father and was now all on her own.

I chased out of my door in an attempt to find Tim. I spotted him on the landing and asked him with some urgency, 'Will you help me to send some flowers to a bereaved friend? I have just read about her father's death in the paper.'

'Yes, of course,' said Tim, 'if you give me the name, address and how much you want to spend.'

'Well,' I said slowly. 'Her name is Miss Mary-Anne Cheyney. Her address is Eaton Square. It doesn't give the address in the paper. Will you look up Sir Robert Cheyney in the telephone book for me?' I asked anxiously.

'I will bring a directory to your room,' said Tim, walking off.

Tim was true to his word, and after much squinting of eyes at the columns of small print, we found, Cheyney, Sir Robert, 135 Eaton Square, London. 460 7200. I quickly wrote down the prized information.

'Eight pounds would make a nice bouquet,' suggested Tim. Without hesitation, I said, 'Make it twenty-eight, and I will give you a cheque.'

'Fine,' said Tim, 'what do you want to put on the card?'

I had forgotten about a card. I felt like telling Mary-Anne how much I loved her, needed her and would be with her to take care of her very soon, but those words seemed inappropriate at this time. I looked at Tim, took a deep breath and said, 'Tim, for the card, say, Mary-Anne, God bless your father. All my love, Michael.'

I turned and stared out of the window before saying to Tim, 'Where is Eaton Square?'

He said, looking as though he meant it, 'I will tell you, but don't you dare attempt to go there. You may only leave here with Dr Chipotski's permission. I'm telling you this for your own good.'

With some reluctance, and using place names that he did not realize meant nothing to me, he said, 'Go straight down the road outside here till you come to Hyde Park Corner, along Knightsbridge to Sloane Street, left on to the Kings Road, take the fourth right and you're in Eaton Square.'

He added, 'It's a very long walk.' With his directions as clear as mud to me, he said, 'I'll send those flowers now,' and left the room.

'Thank you so much,' I called gratefully after him.

On my own again, I thought, I now have Mary-Anne's address and phone number. What a triumph! I then reminded myself of how much I hated the phone as a method of talking to someone. It seemed so impersonal somehow. I needed to see and be with Mary-Anne in order for my words to give their real meaning. I decided I must go and see her just as soon as I was able to. I expected to be allowed out for a walk soon.

My mind wandered round the idea that I might run away to 135 Eaton Square in spite of Tim's severe warning, except that I felt Mary-Anne needed a little time to be with what was left of her relations during this sad time for her. She always used to speak of her father affectionately as Daddy.

A mere glimpsing thought of Mary-Anne shrouded in black, with tears in those so often merrily teasing, laughing eyes made me feel desperately and helplessly unhappy. I put my head in my hands and gently sobbed. I knew that I never wanted to see her like that, ever, ever, ever!

After lunch, when I had sat next to Sue and teased her into smiling, there was a knock at the door and in came the famous Dr Chipotski.

'Good afternoon, Michael. How are you today?' he said, giving me no time to reply before saying, 'Your IQ test was exceptional. This is useful for us to know, but you could in fact join that special society of people with a similar ability.' My immediate uncaring absurd thought was, if that society could put Mary-Anne in my arms for ever, I would join now.

'I want to explain my parallel line treatment,' Dr Chipotski said with no discernable accent, in spite of his possible Russian descent. I decided that he could well have been born in West Nimbrington for all it mattered.

'I'm going to put you on some carbonate salt tablets,

which might reduce your extremes of mood,' he said clearly.

'Will I still be able to laugh and cry, or are they outside your lines?' I asked helplessly.

'Yes, of course,' he replied quickly, 'when I say extreme, I mean your lowest periods, and incidentally it can work for mania.'

I thought, I must not let Mary-Anne near these pills or they might stop the huge pleasure she gives and gets from being high.

The doctor continued in a determined manner. 'It may take several weeks before we see any improvement in you, but I'm optimistic that we will. Indeed, I'm hoping in a few weeks that you will be able to go home for a trial weekend.' He added, 'I have spoken to your wife Clare, and she seems pleased with the idea.'

Quick, quick, Michael! I said to myself as my body started to feel tense. I don't want to go home for the weekend. I want and need to go to Mary-Anne's flat down the road. However, it sounds as though they will only release me in what they consider to be a responsible way, which was back into the 'heart' of my so-called family. What family? A wife I don't know, who seems to cope very well without me. A little son who seems to have been given to a chap called Jake instead of me. To complete my argument, my 'home' in Drillingham I had never seen in my life, and it didn't matter to me if I never did.

Worried and enraged inside, I decided to be brave, and said to Dr Chipotski, 'The only home that matters to me is in London, with a lady I love more than anybody in the world.'

'Where did you meet this girl?' he asked.

'We were both patients together at St Matthews Hospital,' I replied innocently.

'Well, take my advice,' he said firmly. 'You start by going back to your wife and son. You will almost certainly find that you will forget all about your brief hospital romance. You were two people thrown together by illness in an abnormal and temporary situation. You are getting better now, and will soon want to take on your responsibilities in the outside world.'

I was horrified that anyone, but particularly the doctor I respected, could consider my relationship with Mary-Anne as casual, insignificant and something I should end, almost as though it had never happened. I pictured the beautiful smiling Mary-Anne in my mind, and knew that there was no other person in this world that I needed so badly, and there never would be.

8

I could see the weather outside through the window in my comfortable room was getting colder. Last week there were flurries of snow, but it was only light and not persistent.

I believed it to be the month of January, as I watched the many people on the pavement seemingly walk even faster than usual. I noticed some wore heavy-looking coats, thick scarves, woolly hats, boots and gloves. Their clothes made them look fat and ungainly, but helped to cushion the inevitable bump of bodies as they weaved their way in between each other. Protected from the harshest discomfort of a cold winter wind, they each make their journey with some strange sense of purpose known only to themselves.

I was expected to go to Norfolk this weekend with Clare. 'Just for two days, to break you in gently,' Dr Chipotski had said. I had decided that I would go to Drillingham if I had to, in order to be free of this hospital's restrictions on me going to see Mary-Anne rather than Clare.

On Saturday morning I waited in my room for Clare to arrive. I expected her to be punctual, because she had been before. I was apprehensive about the weekend, although my body was feeling much stronger. I still felt uncertain that I was capable of coping with the hazardous world outside my room. I reflected that hospital life was an escape from a thousand and one normal stressful situations that most people accepted as just part of their daily lives. I visualized a few of my worries, such as crossing the road, mingling with strangers, using the

106

phone, escaping media intrusion, spiders, seeing someone crying and getting geographically lost. My ultimate fear was loneliness, which meant to me not having anyone understanding to talk to. In other words, I decided it was like feeling that you had landed on the wrong planet!

Clare arrived in my room only a few minutes late. She was dressed surprisingly informally in a thick brown jersey and well tailored tapered trousers, with just the toe of her high heels visible.

'Hullo, darling,' she said, addressing my cheek with her formal stamp of lipstick. 'Haven't you got a coat? It's freezing outside,' she said with the surprise she needed to distract me from the fact that she had forgotten to bring one.

'I'll be alright in the car,' I said with a gallant undertone. I suddenly thought, is anything of mine in Norfolk? 'Clare, are my clothes at home?' I enquired.

'Of course,' she said indignantly.

'Fine,' I said, grabbing my case. 'Let's go.'

As we started our journey, Clare said we had to travel about one hundred and twenty miles, and that it might take us as much as four hours. I glanced at the Wolseley's speedometer. It went up to one hundred and ten miles an hour. What a waste! I thought.

After two hours and very little conversation, I realized how long and uncomfortable this journey was. Clare, I thought, had great determination to do so much driving just to fetch me. I seemed to be being driven from the sanctuary of my hospital room through the hurly-burly of a foreign land. What was worse, every mile was taking me further from London. How, I thought, am I going to do the journey from Drillingham to Eaton Square? Would Clare lend me 'Daddy's' car, or would I have to steal it? I knew I would get lost on all these strange roads, but never mind, I said to myself, I would not have to put a plan into practice until I had been sent 'home' on a permanent basis.

I had plenty of time to look at the left side of Clare, without her even knowing. I could see and appreciate her small round face and her short straight dark hair. She reminded me slightly of the pictures I had seen of

Japanese girls. I felt with her oriental looks and her small build she would look quite attractive in a kimono, in a dainty way. She was certainly pretty, pleasing and very presentable. Somehow her elaborate heavy make-up and unsmiling motionless expression made her skin look like the painted porcelain that could be seen on a child's doll.

I changed my gaze and stared blankly at the road ahead as I continued to think about my wife, of whom I seemed to know so little. I decided that what she was sadly missing was vibrance, humour and the use of the vital untamed jocular ridicule that I felt needed on occasions to be directed at the straitlaced formalities of life.

My mind gladly changed its focus on to Mary-Anne, as I sat back and closed my eyes. She was a vital, unfettered lady. She had this indefinable magic about her which used to lift me quickly and easily from feeling sad to enjoying and delighting in being alive. I felt no such emotional uplift in Clare's presence.

Mary-Anne, I recalled, would laugh at life or even herself, whereas Clare was kind, observing company, who found laughter a forced exercise. I hoped that later that day I would be able to talk to Clare honestly about our relationship. Did she still love me, I asked myself, or had she stayed with me because of some strange sense of duty? If Clare truly loved me, a thought that I had begun to doubt, then at some stage I was going to hurt her badly. However, I knew that nothing, not even my wife Clare, was going to keep me away from Mary-Anne.

The view from the car window had changed from traffic, people and houses to narrow roads, large ploughed fields and the occasional welcome tree and hedge.

Clare momentarily turned her head towards me and said, 'Michael, we have made such good time that I didn't suggest stopping. We will be at Willowpit in ten minutes. The house is very modern and comfortable. You will like it,' she added as if an order. 'It has four bedrooms and a double garage.' I wondered who slept in the double garage.

After traversing a short bumpy unmade drive, we came to Willowpit farmhouse. I got out of the car, stretched my

108

arms out and breathed some fresh air. My first glimpse at the outside of the house indicated to me, from the clean bright bricks and the new paintwork, that it had only been completed in the last twelve months or so.

Clare led me in through the bright purple front door as I hoped that her choice of colours was more placid inside. To my pleasure, the hall was in bright country colours. I left my case against a wall of a complicatedly patterned yellow wallpaper and was directed to an armchair near a pseudo-electric log fire. What had happened to farm logs, I asked myself.

When I had sat down, I looked round the room at the jumble of modern furniture, meaningless prints of splattered blobs of coloured paint and china knick-knacks. The attention of my eyes was suddenly caught by a row of eight fat owls on the mantelpiece. Some were made of wood, others of basalt, glass or china. They all appeared to be staring at me and saying, 'What are you doing here?' I decided that Clare's first attempt at furnishing a house made me feel a complete stranger in what was supposed to be my home.

Clare called to me from the sitting room door. 'This should be a great day for you. It's the first time we've had you out for months. Do you like what you have seen of the house?'

'Yes, it's very,' I paused in my reply, 'interesting,' I said quickly. 'Where is young David? Has Jake got him?' I asked, trying to sound casual.

Clare indicated from her concerned expression that she considered the Jake situation needed delicate handling. 'Well, yes,' she said, as though it couldn't possibly matter to me. 'I will ring him and get him to bring David round.'

Clare disappeared to another part of the house to phone, although I could see a telephone on a wicker table in the corner of the sitting room not far from where I was sitting.

I spent at least twenty minutes gazing into space and wondering how much of me, if any part at all, belonged here.

Clare returned with a plate of scrambled eggs for both of us for lunch. 'This is all I've had time to do,' she said

109

briskly. 'Sorry I was so long. I couldn't find the eggs.' She continued her unlikely story by saying as though she had forgotten, 'Oh, I rang Jake. He will bring David back to us after lunch.'

We ate our scrambled eggs from trays on our laps in the sitting room. Clare, with another of her commanding sounding statements, said, 'You will like Jake. He is very good to us. Without his help, poor David would have had to do that long car journey.'

Clare had reminded me. 'Thank you for fetching me all that way from the Duke Clinic,' I said gratefully.

'Don't thank me, Michael,' she said. 'What are wives for?' A good question, I thought.

Our plates were cleared away just before the doorbell rang. Clare moved swiftly to answer it. I felt a rush of cold air and heard Clare say, 'Hullo Jake, come in. Michael is in the sitting room.' Then I caught the sound of Clare's whispered words, 'The poor chap is very tired and confused. Try and make allowances.' I didn't think that was a fair description of me, but for Clare's sake I pretended I hadn't heard.

Little David rushed through the door. 'Hullo Daddy,' he said, smiling at me and jumping on my chair. I immediately put my arm round his small body and pulled him closer to me. I couldn't hold back my tears and buried my face in David's jersey. My little son, who I am an inadequate father to, I thought, God help me.

I looked up and saw through my damp eyes the enormous blurred figure of the man I assumed to be my child's part-time nanny.

'Hi, I'm Jake Paddington,' he said, pushing forward his large well-worn, rough-skinned hand. 'How are you?'

'Worse,' I said, because of the insincere tone of the question. Jake withdrew his hand and placed with difficulty his six foot plus, musclebound heap into an armchair.

Clare, who had been watching from the door, said, 'I will get you all a drink,' and disappeared. At this point David seemed bored with his father and slid off my chair onto the carpet, saying, 'Play a game with me, Uncle Jake.' Since when has Jake been David's uncle, I asked myself.

'Jake, have you known Clare and David for long?' I asked speculatively.

'Yes, I'm pleased to say for about a year. I live in the old Manor House next door. Isn't it cold today?' he said, rubbing his hands and obviously feeling a need to change the subject.

I didn't bother to answer, but looked at this red-faced man who could have been a heavyweight boxer of about thirty years old. I tried to judge whether I felt he was a suitable person to encourage to intrude on my life by befriending my wife and son. I knew that my initial feelings of resentment towards Jake were misplaced. I was now aware more than ever before that, if I basically liked Jake, and he for his part had serious intentions towards Clare, it would make my eventual complete escape to Mary-Anne less painful for all concerned. In fact, I concluded, the arrival of Jake on the scene could not have happened at a better time.

Clare returned with three pewter goblets and a red plastic mug on a tray. 'I've brought us all some red wine and some redcurrant squash for David,' she said, giving us each a drink before sinking herself into a well-cushioned sofa opposite Jake.

I sipped my wine, although my hand held tightly round my goblet had acquired a slight tremor, making a spillage on to my trousers seem highly likely.

'It's a nice heavy red,' I commented to Clare.

'Yes, we started the bottle last night,' she said, looking as though she wished she had not spoken.

I must try to make Clare and Jake feel less guilty about their friendship, however intense it may be. That was my immediate thought, after seeing Clare's look of awkwardness. I decided to start by surprising Clare.

'I'm so pleased to have met you today, Jake. I have heard so many nice things about you from Clare. If it was not for the way you help Clare and David, I would be worrying about them all the time.'

At this point, right on cue, Jake developed a smug grin and said cheerfully, 'It's a pleasure for me. I love helping them. It gets very lonely at the Manor. I'm pleased you don't mind me helping them where I can.' Jake paused,

111

and then seemed to realize he had left out one polite remark and said hurriedly, 'I am, of course, very sorry you have been in hospital for so long. I hope you get better soon.'

I now felt that I had successfully sown the seed of approval to their affair. Later, I decided, I would encourage it to grow into a mature and lasting relationship. This would leave me happily free for Mary-Anne, instead of the cruel alternative of leaving Clare and David to struggle through life on their own after my planned desertion. However, I still knew with absolute certainty, that if my hopes for Clare and Jake failed, they could not change my inevitable course and keep me from the girl who was the most important part of my very existence.

Clare appeared very pensive and was looking down at the floor. Unexpectedly she turned her eyes towards me, which I noticed were alert and had gained a sparkle. She seemed to be thanking me.

'I'm pleased you appreciate Jake's kindness to David and me. I was worried you might resent him,' she said, speaking quite openly. 'Sometimes I don't know what I'd do without his moral support when you are not well. Have some more wine,' she said, calling me 'darling' in a refreshed manner.

'Yes, I'd love a little,' I said as I saw her approach my goblet with an almost empty bottle.

Jake was playing a colour brick building game with David. They both seemed to be totally absorbed in it. When Jake had stacked up some bricks, David would give a delighted high-pitched laugh and knock them over with his little hands.

As I sipped my partly filled wine goblet, I noticed that Jake had short curly fair hair, the sort, I assumed, he never had to brush. Clare, I noticed, looked attractive and relaxed in her armchair and was quite content to watch Jake and David at play.

I wondered if Clare still loved me, or did it just suit her to be kind and polite to me for the time being. I wanted Clare to love Jake, not me. She must not depend on me or she would get badly hurt. I decided that I was unlikely to understand Clare's true loyalties until I had left the clinic for good and had spent more time with her. As for my adorable little child David, I felt closer to him each time I saw him. There were warning bells going in my head. I must not get too emotionally close to him, or my planned parting would be desperately painful for both of us. I argued to suit myself that being deserted by a father you barely knew was not so bad if your friendly 'uncle' Jake took over as your Daddy.

Jake looked at his gold watch with its wide brown leather strap, and said in a definite tone, 'Clare, I must go now. I've got the labs to feed.' He stood up and showed me once more what an enormous man he was. He must have to have his clothes hand-made to order, I thought. He turned to me. I felt his facial features indicated kindness, friendliness, but not much brain. 'Very nice to have met you, Michael', he said in a surprisingly high-pitched tenor voice. 'I'll keep an eye on things while you are away. See you next time you come home. You'll have to come and see the Manor.'

'I'd love to,' I said, still trying to work out the extent to which Jake was emotionally involved with Clare. I thought that he might need a very obvious push at some stage to get him to break his bachelor ways in the right direction.

'Bye David,' he said, looking down and smiling at my tidily-dressed son, who was kneeling on the carpet amongst his bricks.

'Bye Uncle Jack. See you tomorrow,' spoke a little content voice.

Jake walked past Clare and said, 'Don't bother to show me out,' and gave her a deliberate reassuring pat on her hand that was resting on her armchair.

Clare leant down and said to David, 'Shall I get Tessa for Daddy?'

'Yes Mummy,' came the small voiced reply from David as his face lit up into a picture of expectant delight.

Clare left the room briskly. I asked David, with his little flat nose and happy baby face, 'Who is Tessa?'

'She's our dog, Daddy. You know.'

I remembered that we used to have a dog. It was a yellow labrador. The next moment the very same dog came into the room and jumped round me with excitement. She soon had her front legs on my lap so that we were nearly able to rub noses.

'Yes, of course I remember this friendly loyal face,' I said, placing my goblet on a side table for safety.

'Tessa certainly remembers you, Michael,' said Clare, clearly surprised by the extent of Tessa's welcome. 'Oh!' she said, 'now she's licking your face. Come on Tessa, sit down.' Tessa lay obediently on the floor, panting very fast but still looking at me intently. While gently stroking Tessa's back as she knelt on the floor beside her, Clare told me, 'Last year Tessa had a litter of puppies. There were five bitches and four dogs. I fell in love with them, and kept two bitches to keep their mum company. Jake had two dogs, and the rest were sold.' Somehow I knew that I was getting very bored with Clare's conversation. I tried to nod and look interested. I contributed the occasional 'Oh really'. Some of Clare's favourite thoughts were clearly enjoying this outing. I strongly surmised, as her confident flow of words continued.

'I have a new thoroughbred. He's a bay gelding. He's sixteen hands and is called Mensorat Willowherb, or Willow for short,' said Clare, looking very pleased with herself. A brief pause for breath allowed me to say quickly, 'Do you hunt, Clare?'

This mention of a horse had reminded me that I was not a keen supporter of traditional fox hunting. I didn't like the type of people who took part, with their pompous dress, whips and spurs. I definitely hated the way some of them treated their horses.

'No,' said Clare firmly, 'Jake and I enjoy eventing and most of all Hunter trials. That twenty acres I told you about is used by us for gun dog training, but it is actually laid out as a small cross-country course. You wouldn't believe it,' she said, grinning broadly, 'but last week I fell headlong off Willow into the water jump; gosh, it was cold!' she giggled. I found it impossible to see what was funny about her predictable story, but for her sake my muscles moved my cheeks to order.

'I will show you the farm and the men next time you come home,' she said, probably sensing her captive audience was going deaf if not to sleep. 'I think you should not try to do too much this first time out.'

I declined Clare's offer to watch television. As an alternative form of entertainment I was handed a farming magazine, which I allowed to lie unopened on my lap. I found myself feeling tired and disinterested in my surroundings. I reflected that it had already been a long and confusing day.

Clare stood up, her black trousers now slightly creased, and said to me while looking at David, who seemed to be trying to eat a brick, 'I will give this little monkey some supper and then pop him to bed. I won't be long.' Quickly understanding his mother, David dropped his brick and followed her out of the room.

I stretched my legs a little, allowing the magazine to slide on to the floor. I then leant forward and turned round each of the beady-eyed owls so that they faced the wall. Now in a completely quiet, unspied-upon setting, I lay back and closed my eyes.

Some time later, my thoughts were brought back into the room by the noise of Clare wheeling a trolley laden with cheese and fruit across the carpet. 'Help yourself,' she said. She was clearly proud of the selection she had chosen. She was looking at the cheeses and smiling.

We both sat quietly while we ate, letting our eyes move slowly over the optional delicacies. Suddenly, without thinking, I said, 'Why should a young girl burn her body with cigarettes?'

'Sorry,' said Clare, mishearing me while her mouth was full of brie and biscuit, 'I didn't catch that.'

'No, it doesn't matter,' I said hastily, remembering almost too late that Clare would not be interested or enlightening about poor Sue's problems. Indeed, as I let my mind move freely, I became sadly aware that Clare, nice as she was, did not have the capacity or the desire to understand my illness. I was sure that she did not tell even her closest friends that I was resident in a psychiatric clinic. She would surely say, 'Oh, but Cynthia, my husband Michael is away on business in the Far East. I'm not sure when he will get back. He rings me from time to time. He sounds very well.'

I thought more carefully and tried to be completely fair

to Clare. She had tried to visit me twice in hospital, which can't have been easy for her. However, I did feel strongly that she had a fear of the part of me that she didn't know, and wanted to pretend it didn't exist. I compensated for my concern about Clare's difficulties by visualizing a day in the future when she would be married to a normal man and I would be living with an abnormal woman.

Clare stood up purposefully and started to stack the plates and take out the trolley. 'Come with me, Michael,' she said gently, 'and I will show you the bedrooms and bathroom.'

As I followed Clare up the stairs, it occurred to me with some alarm that I just might be invited to sleep with my wife. I decided that if I couldn't manage to make love at the moment with Mary-Anne, I certainly was not going to try to succeed with Clare. Anyway, the more negative I was about sex the more inviting Jake would become.

I was shown the main bedroom, which had two single beds in it, divided by a bedside table with a blue shaded lamp on it. Clare found me my pyjamas and pointed out my motley collection of clothes in the room next door. The bathroom, in sickly pink, reminded me to take some of my amazing collection of prescribed coloured pills.

When we were both tucked up comfortably in separate beds, Clare said, 'Goodnight darling,' as though out of habit, and switched out the light. I lay on my back and looked into the blackness of the unlit room. I imagined that Clare would look small, neat and trim with no clothes on, just as she did when fully dressed. I simply couldn't remember, but I was not too concerned. She was to be Jake's wife and definitely not mine.

I thought slowly as the sleeping pills increasingly influenced me. They seemed to keep my mind on a repetitive line of enquiry. There was obviously living proof that I had successfully made love to Clare about five years ago. What had happened to her sex life since? I knew the pictures of my past were blurred and distorted by time, tablets and treatments. I concluded they were best left like that, as I started to dream of my future with Mary-Anne.

I leant back in my chair and rested my feet in my usual manner on the edge of the bed. I definitely felt more relaxed in my small familiar room at the clinic than I had done in the strange modern house which was home to Clare and David.

Today Clare, without a word of complaint about the distance, completed the long drive with me from Willow-pit Farm to the Duke Clinic. I had tried to memorize the route we took to help me on a future solo trip, but I lost track of place names after half an hour. I decided I would try to remember road numbers instead on the next journey to Norfolk.

There was an unexpected knock on my door and Dr Chipotski, looking cheerful, came through the door. He wore his dark city suit wth a bright red and white spotted tie. I thought he looked more like a well-dressed merchant banker than psychiatrist.

'Hullo Michael, did you have a good weekend at home?' he asked enthusiastically.

'Yes I did, thank you,' I replied.

'How did you get on with your wife?' he asked.

'Very well,' I said, remembering that I now had discovered a positive plan to enable my pending escape from Clare and Drillingham to be as painless as I thought possible.

'Well, I told you only the other day,' said the doctor, hands on hips and beaming with self-satisfaction, 'that the relationship you had with another patient was a spur of the moment affair which was best forgotten. It sounds to me as though you and your wife and son will soon be one happy family again.'

Thinking it was perfect timing, I asked Dr Chipotski in a quiet pleading voice, 'When will you allow me to go home for good?' He dropped one hand by his side and moved the other to caress his chin.

'Well,' he said, pausing for thought, 'you have made good progress. The new salt tablets must have started to work quickly in your case.' After a further pause, he looked straight at me and said in an absolute manner, 'If you continue to make progress this week, then next weekend is a very strong possibility.'

'That is good news. Thank you,' I said freely, knowing the 'Irishness' of my situation. The sooner I went back to Norfolk, the sooner I would be in London.

That evening, thoroughly keyed up by the news that I might be allowed out soon, I went looking for Tim instead of waiting for him. I walked the full length of the landing without success. However, it was not Tim that I wanted particularly. It was the use of a telephone that I needed so badly. I looked into Sister's office. She noticed me and said, 'What can I do for you, Michael?'

'Er . . . I just,' I said, hesitating because I wanted to make this call in private, 'wanted to make a quick phone call please, Sister.'

'Yes, you can. Do you know the number?' she asked, putting her hand on a pile of directories.

'Yes, I've got it written down,' I said as I showed Sister, standing in her immacutely starched and ironed uniform, a small ball of crumpled paper in the palm of my hand.

'Use this phone on my desk,' she requested, and pointed to the only phone on her desk.

I lifted the receiver and dialled the number just as Sister appeared to be leaving. Instead Dr Chipotski came in and joined her at the precise moment that I heard the phone start to ring in what I hoped was Mary-Anne's flat. I was panic-stricken. I knew Dr Chipotski would not let me go home if he thought that I had not forgotten about my tmeporary hospital affair, as he called it. What was I going to say, I wondered, if Mary-Anne answered, that could be harmlessly overheard? A restrained 'Hullo,' sounded in my ear. My God, it's her, I said to myself with surprise. I recognized just one word from her voice immediately and then took fright and banged the receiver back on the phone. Both Sister and Dr Chipotski looked round at me.

Sister said, looking perplexed, 'That was a very quick call, Michael.'

'Oh, it was a wrong number,' I tried to say casually but didn't succeed. I said a very awkward, 'Thank you,' as I walked shakily out of Sister's office and returned to my room.

I didn't think the phone call was wasted. I now thought I knew that Mary-Anne was definitely living at 35 Eaton Square. As I slowly ambled round my room, I felt invigorated and spurred on because I had heard one word from the unique voice. I decided with even greater determination that I would see her as soon as I possibly could, but that I would humour Dr Chipotski until the end of the week so that I was discharged a free man. I did not want a recurrence of further police or any other investigations into where I might have gone. I knew, of course, that I would only be discharged if it was seen to be into the caring hands of my wife Clare. So be it, I thought with the indications of a smile beginning to appear on my face.

I lay in bed that evening thinking about Mary-Anne, and my young son David, whom I was most loathe to abandon. I knew, however, that I had no other choice. Mary-Anne would never want children. She and I were both too irresponsible to guide and protect a child. If she was looking after David she would probably buy him an enormously powerful motorbike, like a 650 Triumph Thunderbird, for his fifth birthday, thinking he would have hours of fun with it. She might even give him champagne on his cornflakes as part of his education for life. She would mean well, but not consider the risks her ideas involved. 'My darling Mary-Anne, we won't have children, but we will always have each other,' I mumbled almost silently into my pillow as the god of sleep finally claimed me.

3.

On Friday night I was told by Sister that I could go home and that Clare would pick me up before lunch tomorrow. I was delighted, and went straight to Sue's room to give her my good wishes. Although I felt sure I was ignorant of the reasons behind Sue's peculiar cigarette stubbing behaviour, I decided to appeal to her as a friend for the last time.

'Sue,' I said, while noticing no additional scars on her face, 'Sue, you have a beautiful face and a beautiful body.

119

Beauty should never be discoloured.' I realized that I was losing my way, and from Sue's smiling face, achieving nothing. I gently but deliberately kissed the scar on her cheek and said, 'Take care,' rather uselessly before leaving her room.

At midmorning on Saturday, Clare arrived in my room with two boxes of chocolates. She stood near me wearing her black trousers, topped with a black jersey, indeed, she was dressed entirely in black. She looked to me completely ready to do a robbery at midnight. I gave the chocolates to Sister and Tim. They both seemed delighted. I just hoped their pleasure was not being shown because of my impending absence.

The Wolseley, with Clare's careful handling, soon had us back to Willowpit Farm. I had spent much of the journey thinking, 'Gosh, I'm out in the big wide world,' and then wondering, as I watched some of the appparent chaos of life from the car window, whether I would ever cope. I knew that if I hadn't got my firm resolution to return to London as soon as possible I would have felt even less confident.

I sat in the sitting room in what seemed to have become 'my chair'. I noticed the wretched owls had done an about turn as the lady in black gave me a cup of tea.

'On Monday I will show you round the farm, and we are all invited to lunch with Jake,' she said in an unquestionable way.

'Yes, fine,' I said, trying to be as accommodating as possible, 'that would be nice.'

On Monday morning there was some low-lying mist in the freezing air, so Clare and I were equipped with wellington boots and thick jackets for our farm walk. Clare led the way, and took us through mud and water towards a Dutch barn partly filled with straw.

'Oh, that's bedding for Willow. It's cheaper to make it than buy it,' she said, to satisfy what curiosity I might have had about providing stock bedding on a purely arable farm.

In the barn there were two men replacing shares on a three-furrow plough. Clare introduced me; 'Tom and Don, this is my husband, Mr Simpson.'

An unexpected chorus of 'Pleased to meet you, I'm sure,' followed. I went back to my farming days, and said to Tom, who wore a cloth cap, a navy blue boiler suit and who seemed to be even shorter than Clare, 'Do you get a lot of wear on this ground?'

'We certainly do, Mr Simpson. I reckon it's all them stones,' said Tom, looking short of a few teeth as he gave me a broad grin. I turned to the larger bald-headed man Don, who was halfway through a droopy self-rolled cigarette.

'Have you much more to plough?' I asked.

'Only about fifteen acres, but there's no hurry. It's too cold for any bugger to grow in this weather, even old Tom 'ere! Ain't that right, Tom?' Don laughed heartily at his own joke, and Tom nodded in amusement. We smiled. We were pleased to see the men were happy.

Clare said to the men, 'See you later,' and turned, encouraging me to follow her to a small block of three stables. There was a large heap of horse manure at one end of the building which looked untidy. Clare went straight to the stable that had a fine horse's head sticking out over the bottom door. 'This is my beauty,' she said, stroking the soft brown hair on Willow's neck. He seemed to be a strong good-looking horse to me.

'How did he get the same first name as the farm?' I asked.

'Just a lucky coincidence,' she said, 'it means to me that he has always belonged here. Now Michael, why don't you look at some of the fields while I go for a ride on Willow? Let's meet at Jake's for lunch. You'll find it alright,' she said clearly and firmly. Then, pointing into the distance, she said, 'All the fields behind the barn along the roadside are ours. I think they are all in early drilled wheat.' It was another of those moments when agreeing with Clare was the easist thing to do, so I said, 'Have a good ride,' and started to walk the way I'd been directed.

It was quiet and peaceful strolling across the fields, if a little cold and muddy. I could see the part ploughed field across the road. There were still a few flecks of yellow stubble standing after the burn at harvest time. I could feel my memory of my year spent on a farm coming back to me. I looked down at the young green six-inch-high grass-like plants and checked the auricles on some of them. I soon realized this early drilled wheat as described by Clare was in fact barley.

I remembered I was to go back at about this time for lunch at the Manor House. Apparently David was already there in the dubious care of Jake's alcoholic housekeeper. As I made my way slowly towards the house I decided I would think up an excuse to borrow Clare's car after lunch and head for London. What about, 'May I go for a short drive? I think it might do me good. I haven't driven a car for such a long time.' I tried the words on myself. No! I thought, It sounds too risky for 'Daddy's present'. I kept endeavouring to think of some more inspired words.

Outside the house I discarded my muddy boots. I walked into the deserted sitting room, having temporarily forgotten where I had left my shoes. I sat on the arm of the settee and found my mind wandering away from my lost shoes and on to my planned little family of three. I remembered being surprised yesterday when Clare said that Jake basically managed Willowpit Farm. There seemed very little that Jake didn't manage round here. I felt more and more that it was only a question of time before Clare and David would move in with Jake. The sooner I moved to London, the quicker this would happen, I thought. So I supported in my mind my decision to go this afternoon. I also reaffirmed to myself my earlier decision not to tell Clare that my entire life revolved round another woman until I knew that I never needed to return to Willowpit Farm again.

Tessa was sniffing my trouserleg and aimlessly wagging her tail. I stroked the top of her head and said, 'Tessa, my girl, where are my shoes?' I stood up and walked upstairs towards the bedroom, thinking they might be in a cupboard or perhaps still on the floor beside my bed. As I approached the closed door that led to the bedroom, I was amazed to be able to hear the muffled sound of two people talking. After a moment I could not fail to recognize the amicable noises and whispered words as belonging to Clare and Jake. I crept carefully and silently away, arriving downstairs in my stockinged feet. Tessa was pleased to see me, even after a five minute parting.

'Tessa,' I said quietly and positively, 'this is certainly the day to go to London!' I gave her a big pat on the back. I then slid my feet once more into my muddy boots and wandered towards the Manor, wondering what my host, who had displayed a rather blatant choice of behaviour, had arranged for my lunch in his absence?

The Manor House was an imposing property. The front door was answered by a strange woman who one could only describe as a pathetic mess. She had curly unkempt grey-brown hair, a red face and unpleasantly large eyes. She was dreadfully overweight, and her clothes were no more than rags, including her pair of grubby motheaten slippers. In her right hand, to my surprise, she was holding David's arm.

'Hullo Daddy,' said David cheerfully. I smiled at him. Then I looked at the lady's glazed expression and said, 'I believe Mr Jake Paddington is expecting me for lunch. I'm Michael Simpson, David's father.' Had any of my words been absorbed by my latest and most unusual of acquaintances, I wondered?

'You had better come in then,' she said, turning to indicate my entrance. I pulled off my boots and made my way forward.

The inside of the Manor House was beamed with oak and elm. It was a magnificent sight. I asked David, 'Do you like this house better than Willowpit?'

He looked at me and said guardedly, 'A little bit better, Daddy.'

'Good,' I said, leaving the poor child confused.

I noticed the middle-aged soak had disappeared. In the dining room the table was laid for four people, with silver cutlery and candlesticks. I felt madly underdressed if this was our setting for lunch.

Perfectly dressed and walking into the room from another direction came a totally unruffled Clare. 'I'm sorry if you have been waiting for me, but Willow was in a very stubborn mood this morning.' I was reminded immediately that I had seen Willow still in his box, looking as though he hadn't been moved, let alone exercised, when I walked back home from the fields.

'Oh Michael, you've got no shoes on,' said Clare as though I had let her down badly, 'I left them by the front door all ready for you.'

'Sorry, I couldn't find them,' I said casually with Clare's penetrating eyes looking questioningly at me. 'I just glanced in the hall and then decided to come over in my boots,' I said, hoping to relieve her anxiety. No longer looking worried, Clare said, 'Well done, Michael. Why do shoes matter anyway?' I realized that I agreed with her remark but that she didn't agree with it herself. I looked at her expensively chosen black patent high heels and thought that she would lose a lot of height and elegance without them.

Clare, behaving as though she was in her own home, poured me a dry sherry from a large cut glass decanter and gave David a lemonade from a bottle she found in the sideboard. Then saying, 'I must check the lunch,' and within the restrictions imposed by her tight-fitting navy blue suit, she left the room in a series of tiny fast moving steps.

Jake soon appeared, dressed in a smart tweed jacket, fashionable mole skin trousers and brown leather hacking boots. In spite of an unruffled calm look about him, he also felt it necessary to clarify his morning's activities. 'I've just done a filthy job shovelling about five tons of dusty wheat into an auger. The last load is always a fiddle to pick up cleanly,' he said, all the time concentrating his eyes on a glass tumbler on the sideboard that he was filling with a generous measure of Scotch. I had not realized until that moment what a remarkably good liar Jake was.

Clare returned to the dining room, her shoes making rapid distracting banging noises as she briskly moved towards the table set on a hard wood floor.

'Hullo Jake, did you have a good morning?' she said as though she had not met him since yesterday.

'Very productive,' he replied in an offhand manner. An honest remark at last, I thought.

The four of us were seated when the housekeeper, covering up much disarray of grubby clothing with the help of a smart apron, served us all with fish and chips with great expertise. We each received our vegetables with silver service correctly over our left shoulder.

David said, to my surprise, 'Auntie Jessie, can I have some tomato sauce?'

'Yes, David,' said the housekeeper, and quietly departed in her slippered feet towards the kitchen while I tried to work out the implications of David's words. That extraordinarily unfortunate-looking woman was possibly Jake's sister! It was all too confusing. I decided that I would ask Clare at another time.

I realized that I was acquiring a slight tremor in my hands as I searched my mind for the best words to use when asking Clare if I could use her car. Then good fortune came my way as Clare gave me the perfect opportunity. She said in a fed-up voice, 'I'm supposed to be picking my meat order up from the shops this afternoon, but I don't think that I will have time.' While she spoke she looked in vain at the inattentive Jake. She tried again and said more clearly, 'I want to ride Willow round the cross-country course a couple of times, so I won't have time to go to the butcher.' I thought to myself, if I had believed all that I'd heard about Willow's exercising today, the poor chap would be a very overworked horse. I could see him by tonight, covered in white frothy sweat, walking stiffly and with his head hung down.

Before Jake had a chance to feel sufficiently pressured by Clare so that he felt committed to help her out, I said in my most casual voice, 'Clare, I will willingly fetch your meat for you. A short drive would do me good.'

Clare thought for a moment and then said, 'Fine, Michael, you go out of the gate and turn left. Just follow the road for three miles. It winds a bit. You will see the shops on both sides of the road. The butcher is halfway down on the right. That would be a great help, but do drive carefully.'

After some unnecessarily delicately served balls of perfectly ordinary vanilla ice cream, I had to listen to some more plans for Willow from Clare, which included, 'If he shies at a fence I shall use my whip,' and 'I think his oat ration is far too high.' I more than happily excused myself and left the room.

9

1.

I was soon inside the leathered comfort of the shiny dark blue Wolseley. I was eager to get started and on my way to Mary-Anne. I had found my shoes outside the front door and what was left of my chequebook from my jacket pocket. I had to admit to myself that I felt apprehensive and confused as I began my journey.

I deliberately turned right out of the gate because the butcher's shop was the very last place that I wanted to go. I noticed that I only had less than half a tank of petrol. I knew I had one cheque left for a fill-up.

My control over the car was no more confident than on that extraordinary trip in a Mini that I made with my adorable but less than helpful co-driver, Mary-Anne. I wished she was with me now. Never mind, I thought, gripping my hands even more tightly round the wheel, in just a few hours we will be together.

I drove Clare's smart blue car through places I did not remember. However, when I came to the town of Diss, I felt reassured that I was on the same road that Clare had used when taking me to the clinic. I filled up with petrol and prayed that I would not need any more before I arrived at Eaton Square.

Somewhere on the outskirts of Diss I seemed to have drifted off the main road and found myself travelling down narrow, winding lanes with road signs that meant nothing at all to me. I felt it was a cold, bright, pleasant afternoon for people who liked driving. I didn't, and found concentrating on the road ahead, or behind for that matter, extremely difficult. I was confident that I was travelling south, which led me to believe that after a few more s-bends and humpback bridges I would find myself on the main road to Ipswich.

I didn't like driving fast, because it made the scenery change too quickly for me. I preferred to meander along at a gentle pace, giving myself time to think how pleased I was to have left Willowpit Farm and now be heading for real love and sanity. There was a loud bang type noise, and the car stopped abruptly. I pushed myself back in my seat and looked carefully through the windscreen. I found that I could see far too close to me a large oval-topped yellow mass, which could have been an unusually solid lump of fog or, more likely, one of those unavoidable, slow-moving road sweepers. I could see a cross-looking man in blue overalls walking back down the side of the yellow monster towards me.

I got out of the Wolseley feeling slightly shaken, knowing that I must have damaged Clare's car. However, I was much more concerned and upset to realize that I was not going to be with Mary-Anne tonight.

It quickly became obvious that the driver of the large yellow lorry had something to say when, before I could ask him which was the Ipswich road, he said fiercely, 'Why don't you look where you're bloody going? You shouldn't be driving a sodding car if you can't see a bloody great road sweeper!'

I glanced at the broken glass and misshaped panels at the front of Clare's car and tried to ignore the lorry driver's steady flow of abuse. Then I had had enough and turned to the overalls so full of destructive criticism and said, 'What a damn silly place to park!'

He quickly retorted, 'I was not parked, I was brushing slowly.'

The driver looked at the Wolseley's very unhappy, distorted front end and then stated the obvious, 'Your car will need to go to a garage. There's one up the road.'

'Can you give me a lift?' I said, thinking Clare's car would not start.

The driver looked exasperated and said forcefully, 'This, my friend, is a County Council Road Sweeper, and not a bloody taxi! Thank your lucky stars, Sonny Jim,' he said crossly, pointing a well-oiled finger at me, 'that you don't seem to have damaged my vehicle. So as far as I'm concerned, this accident never happened.' He started to walk away from me towards his cab door, and as he did, turned and said, still maintaining his hostile manner, 'I will now carry on brushing until some other prat like you thinks I'm invisible.'

I was in a state of panic because my vital plans to see Mary-Anne had gone wrong and I was concerned about the inevitable forthcoming wrath of my wife. I managed to drive Clare's battered car past my 'friend' in the slow-moving yellow lorry and find the garage that he had mentioned. East Road Garage had two petrol pumps and a large old shed standing behind them. I parked the Wolseley and asked the solitary figure of a pump attendant if I could make a reverse charge call on his phone. As he showed me the phone, just inside the shed full of damaged cars, he glanced at the front of Clare's car and said, 'Had a bit of a shunt, mate?'

I saved my sarcasm and just said, 'Yes.'

'You won't be going anywhere in that!' he added as I picked up the receiver and dialled the operator. I thought it might be Dawn who answered.

Soon I was talking to Clare, or rather she to me. 'Where the hell are you? You've been hours. You only had to go three miles down the road to the butcher. You have been gone over two hours!' There was a pause, and I knew that I was now allowed, indeed expected, to explain my use of time.

I said cheerfully, 'I was getting you a special present of those world-famous Ipswich sausages.' I was quite pleased with my spur of the moment lie, when the words, 'Where are you now?' came down the phone from Clare's increasingly cross voice.

'Oh, I'm at a small garage called East Road Garage, near the town of Diss,' I said casually.

Clare was clearly getting impatient with my apparent inability to explain myself as she said loudly, 'That's over thirty miles away! Why are you at a garage? You better not have damaged my Wolseley! Well?'

'Just a slight bump,' I said gently, 'nothing a little metal bending won't put right.'

'You bastard,' she said, 'you drive off for no good reason in my car, and then crash it! Michael, I have had just about enough of you. You will never drive my car again!'

'Shall I come back by taxi? Will you pay for it?' I asked humbly, but thinking Clare was badly over-reacting to the situation.

'You ought to have to walk!' she retorted and then paused before saying, 'I will use Jake's Land Rover and fetch you. I want to see the state of my car after your complete incompetence. I can't trust you with anything!' There was an abrupt click sound in my ear, followed by the dialling tone.

It was starting to get dark and colder as Clare arrived at the garage in the canvas-topped Land Rover. She strutted across the forecourt to her car, and did not even acknowledge me standing in the cold waiting for her. She was dressed in her jodhpurs and knee-length riding boots. I quite expected from the earlier clear indication of her mood that she would be carrying Willow's whip especially to use on me.

'My God!' she exclaimed, 'what an appalling mess! What will Daddy say?' She turned and looked at me harshly as if to say, you miserable creature, you haven't heard the last of this! 'Get in the Land Rover,' she yelled at me, just as she might have spoken to Tessa.

While Clare talked to the garage man I sat in the Land Rover and wondered why Clare did not show a more caring attitude to me. After a crash, I thought, even if you felt your car was infinitely more important to you than the driver, it was at least polite to ask if he was injured in any way. Instead, all Clare seemed to want to do was to make up for the injuries she guessed I hadn't received in the crash by hurting me unnecessarily with her thoughtless verbal abuse. I did not remember this side of Clare's nature.

The journey home, rattling through the darkened lanes, was not pleasant. Clare was still unbelievably angry. She chose the opportunity to throw unkind remarks at me that must have been kindling inside her for months.

'Why do you think I like Jake? He's a real man instead

of a wimp like you. He isn't pathetically ill and crying that he is misunderstood as you are most of the time.' The expression on Clare's face as she spoke showed cold hard satisfaction from the words and a clear need to continue. 'What sort of life do you think it is for me being married to a feeble, tremoring, impotent man? Well, I can tell you, it is no life at all! Since you have been at home we have slept in the same room, but we might as well have been in separate houses! You never give me a kiss or a cuddle even. You simply don't care about anyone except yourself. Well, Michael, when we get home there are going to be a few changes!'

'I do care about you, Clare,' I said weakly but honestly in my defence. 'I just don't feel emotionally demonstrative at the moment, and your shouting at me does not help matters. Try and remember that I have just got out of a car crash,' I said, hoping for some understanding.

'How could I forget, you idiot!' she shouted angrily.

Clare pulled into Willowpit Farm saying, 'Jake won't need this Land Rover tonight. He's gone out. Right, Michael, you and I are going straight to bed,' Clare ordered. 'David is at the Manor with Jessie.'

'Is Jessie Jake's sister?' I asked as we walked through the dimly-lit front door.

'Yes,' said Clare, 'she owns half the estate, but is too stupid with drink to be able to help run it.' How convenient for Jake, I though with a restrained smile.

'Why do you want to go straight to bed?' I asked Clare with apparent innocence.

'Because I am going to show you something for the last time, and I want to see if you are a man or a mouse,' she said firmly. I realized that I was in very deep trouble. I had never seen Clare like this before. Sex and bed had always been words she rarely used. I was worried that she might be expecting an erotic performance from me that I knew I didn't even like trying to provide. I considered that perhaps right now I was going to have to tell her about Mary-Anne. I decided to see what she was planning first.

I was soon ordered into the bedroom by Clare and told to undress, while she stormed into the bathroom and slammed the door. I removed my jacket and hung it on the back of a chair. I stood a few paces away from the bed and waited. After just a moment Clare came in, wearing a yellow bathrobe and slippers.

'Why aren't you undressed,' she said indignantly, while standing quite close to me. I reluctantly and yet stubbornly unbuttoned the top of my shirt. 'Take your trousers off,' she yelled. I refused to move, and looked at her defiantly.

Clare, when certain I was looking, let her bathrobe slide off her slender shoulders onto the floor, as though she was saying goodbye to a mink coat that she was sorry to lose. She revealed her total nakedness. I saw that she was, as I had thought, as neat and trim in the flesh as she appeared to be when fully dressed. To me, her body was not an object for sex. It was, I considered, merely the functional pink-skinned covered framework that every person required in some shape or another.

Clare, with her hands behind her head, wiggled her small gently curved bottom and said, 'Come on, you dumb sexless oaf. Am I not sexy enough for his lordship's taste tonight?'

I stayed still with my back towards the cupboard, only a few feet away from the end of the bed. I felt embarrassed, fed up with her sick behaviour and about at the point where verbal explosions were inevitable.

Clare would not accept defeat easily, and continued her act with a contortion of her limbs that I had not seen before. She kept her feet on the ground and arched her back so that her head and hands were on the edge of the bottom of the bed. She then opened her knees in front of me, and said clearly, in spite of her head facing the ceiling, 'What do you think of that, you impotent toerag?'

I had taken enough of this little girl's taunting and teasing. I knew that I had no intention of making love to her, so I shouted as loudly as I could, 'Stop it, Clare! Put your bathrobe on this minute! I don't want to do it at the moment. Why can't you understand? I'm in love with another woman!'

Clare stood up, clutching her robe. She looked so disgusted with me, I thought she was going to spit in my face. Instead, she yelled at the top of her voice, 'The hell you are! You just can't tell the truth. You don't fancy your own bloody wife! You have hurt me more deeply than you will ever know, Michael Simpson, but you never will again! Leaving you to rot with your shakes, pains and pathetic impotence will now be an easy pleasure! Tonight I will sleep in the spare room. Tomorrow I will move in with Jake permanently!'

Now Clare's face was red with anger, and the belt round her bathrobe was tied in a knot so tight that I didn't think it would ever come undone. I knew that I had deeply offended her by my complete lack of effort, but she wouldn't believe that all my feelings were directed towards another woman.

Clare angrily stamped her little feet as she made her way out of the bedroom and gave me her parting bad-tempered words as the curtain fell on her polished performance, 'I hope I'll never see you again!' She slammed the door behind her to create extra effect, but I was just pleased to know it was shut.

As I stood alone in the bedroom, I felt so pent up that I had a strong desire to smash something. I clenched my fists and paced round and round on a small area of carpet until I decided that I could just about control my feelings. I sat on the edge of my bed and asked myself, why did Clare choose to do this to me tonight? Perhaps it made leaving me for Jake that much easier for her? I didn't think I would ever know, but I could understand her distressed and angry behaviour at being totally rejected by me, whatever the circumstances. Although I secretly believed her final break from me to Jake relied on the appropriate cause for an enormous row to appear or be created. Clare, I felt, had got what she wanted even though the rejection she had anticipated had hurt her female pride.

The next morning I woke early with a still vivid picture of my naked wife yelling at me in my mind. As I got dressed, I was trying to think of another way to get to London. I realized that I had no money.

When I got downstairs, I found Clare trying to carry a suitcase towards the front door. Her dark hair was uncombed, and she hadn't bothered with makeup.

'I will be taking Tessa. You will never remember to feed her!' she said, avoiding looking at me. She fought her way out of the house with her heavy case as though there was some emergency that she had to go and deal with. Was she frightened of me or herself, I wondered. The door was slammed shut, and I found myself left standing alone in Clare's crazy little decorated world of meaningless small modern objects. The owls, the pictures, the china and the tourist trophies were all irritating distractions to me. I thought I would stuff them in a suitcase later.

It looked a bright and crisp day outside. How do I get to Mary-Anne? I asked myself. I knew only too well that I had no car and no money. I didn't think that Clare or Jake would feel like helping me. I decided to go and see Don and Tom. They might have some ideas about transport to London.

I put on a thick coat and boots, and then strutted through the light watery mud that led towards the dutch barn. I could soon see Don's bald head.

'Good morning, Don,' I said to attract his attention.

'Morning, Mr Simpson,' Don said as he sat on a straw bale and spoke through a mouthful of sandwich.

'Sorry to disturb your breakfast, Don. Where's young Tom today?' I enquired out of interest.

'Oh, 'ee be 'aving 'is docky in Mrs Simpson's tack room.'

'Why?' I asked.

'Oh, 'ee's got a cold fried egg 'is Misses done for 'is sandwich. 'Ee's warmin' it up on the electric fire.'

'Really,' I said, trying not to imagine the well-handled end product.

Behind Don's bale stood the ninety horsepower Massey Ferguson tractor with a three-furrow reversible plough hitched to it. A strange and desperate thought occurred to me.

'Don,' I said, 'what is my best way to get to London?'

'Well,' said Don, 'I wouldn't start from 'ere!' He doubled up with a sandwich-spitting chuckle.

'Don, have you ever been out of Drillingham?' I asked out of curiosity.

'Not since moy Misses 'ad all 'er teeth art. They done it in Norwich about ten year back. She did it for 'er job, see?'

133

I didn't see, and I couldn't imagine what her job was! I was more interested in my idea of trying the large red tractor.

'Don,' I said, 'I'd like to do some ploughing to help you out.'

'You don't 'ave to do that, Mr Simpson. I'll get it done afore the last frost,' he said, sounding slightly offended.

'No, Don,' I said, hoping to dispel the thought that I was in any way criticising his speed of work. 'I'd like to do a few acres just to keep my hand in.'

Don looked a little happier and said, 'If you say so, Mr Simpson. She's filled up and ready to go.'

I opened the metal-framed canvas door and sat proudly on the large adjustable seat. As I gripped the steering wheel, it felt like fun and brought back happy memories. I noticed a dead rabbit near the clutch pedal and held it out of the door by its back legs.

Do you want this, Don?' I asked.

'Yes, that's mine,' he said, tucking it inside the front of his coat.

I shut the door, pressed the stop button, turned the ignition key and the engine came to life! What a lovely magnificent noise, I thought, as diesel fumes pulsated their way through the exhaust pipe. I lifted the plough on the hydraulics and then indicated to Don with a waving hand that I was off, to enable him to move the straw bale, his docky bag and his charming idle self.

I felt pleased to be back in a tractor as I drove slowly down the road to the field gateway. Once in the field I reversed the plough into the hedge, lowered it to the ground, then swiftly disconnected the lift arms and the top pin. I drove the tractor forwards a few yards. 'Hurray,' I called out as I saw the tractor and I were free. Back on the road, I had to go the same way as the day before. In top gear I drove past the Manor House, wondering as I went if Clare now found Jake an even more enjoyable mate after my pathetic performance last night. I hoped for my sake that they were at least preoccupied enough not to feel the need to gaze out of their windows.

The tractor felt as though it was going very fast, but its top speed was only about fifteen miles an hour. I said to myself, Mary Anne here I come, nothing will stop me now! I believed that I could even push a roadsweeper with a none-too-friendly driver into the ditch.

I drove for hour after hour, constantly pulling into the side of the road to allow queues of faster traffic to pass me. I wondered why everyone seemed in such a desperate hurry. I didn't like the angry faces as people turned their heads to look at me with disapproval, before racing past me in their one-hundred-mile-an-hour cars.

In spite of the traffic, the noise and the general chaos of overcrowded streets, it was a beautiful day. The sun was shining, and I noticed that a few daffodils had started to flower, indicating that at least they thought spring was upon us.

'An 'old boy' caught my eye as I bumbled along. He was leaning on a hoe in his front garden, quite content to watch the world and his wife rush around while he stood perfectly still. He was possibly thinking, they're a silly lot of buggers, and he would probably have been right. I could not help but be reminded of Joe, the 'reverend' scout. I wondered if he was as jovial as ever and still defending his roses from any other plant life. I remember that he used to use his hoe in such a wild manner that he seemed to club the weeds into submission.

I decided that I was just going to sit on this machine until I got to Eaton Square. Boredom, food, traffic, but nothing was going to stop me. If after about one hundred and fifty miles, a calculation based on Don's remark 'she's filled up', I found that I needed fuel, I would try and find a sympathetic farmer. Perhaps I'd give him my coat if necessary or a bit off the tractor I didn't need, such as the front weights, the lift arms or even the cab.

I managed to stay on the main road through Diss and avoided all dogs, prams, people and roadsweepers. After moments of confusion in my mind concerning my directions I found myself on the A11, a road I remembered Clare bringing me up in her Wolseley. At last the traffic and turmoil seemed reduced as I found myself happily making progress up the inside lane. I felt fortunate now because there were two lanes, and people could overtake me easily. I thought this road was such a big road that it must lead to 'the big city'. I smiled to myself. After six hours driving and with still half a tank of diesel, I felt that I was on the right road and definitely going to make it!

My optimism was soon shattered as a police car slowly overtook me and signalled to me to pull over on to the grass verge and stop. One uniformed policeman examined the outside of the tractor while the other, a red-faced Sergeant, opened the cab door and said, 'Where do you think you are going?'

I got out on to the ground and said, 'London, Sergeant.'

'Going to do a little ploughing in Regents Park, are we?' he said in a very sarcastic voice.

I felt very annoyed at being stopped, and wondered what the police thought I'd done wrong. The tall Sergeant seemed young, keen and determined to find fault. I noticed that he had an acne-scarred face, so without thinking I said, 'Do you have an older brother called Dave?'

He looked surprised and said angrily, 'If you don't shut up I'll book you for the lot.'

'What do you mean?' I said, having no idea what he was talking about any more than he understood why I related his acne to his non-existent brother Dave.

The Sergeant called to his mate, who, from his position, seemed to be having a sleep under the back axle. 'Ray, I'm going to question this joyrider, come and write it all down.' Gathered in a huddle at the edge of the road he said, 'Name and address?'

'Michael Simpson, and temporarily Drillingham, Norfolk,' I replied.

'Occupation?'

'Staying alive,' I said.

'Put down none,' he said inconsiderately. 'Did you drive this farm machine from Norfolk today?' he asked, looking as though he was ready to pounce with satisfaction on my answer.

'Yes,' I said proudly.

'Book him for no road fund licence, Ray. Six miles a week is the limit, and you have managed to exceed it by about seventy miles already this week,' he said, delighted to prove I was a lawbreaker. He persisted in his questioning, hoping perhaps for more serious charges. 'Are you driving this tractor with the owner's consent?'

I struggled with the words for my reply, 'Well, no, but my wife or perhaps more accurately my ex-wife's father owns it, or at least I think he does. Why, do you want to buy it? You can have it for nothing when I get to London.'

The Sergeant, infuriated by my flippant dithering attitude, said crossly, 'Book him for stealing the tractor.' Ray then volunteered that there were no indicators, no rear number plates, and there was a pool of hot oil on the grass. The Sergeant, so triumphant at having solved his case and found another criminal, didn't listen to Ray and quickly bundled me into his car.

They took me to a nearby police station, which seemed dark and disorganized, and prepared a charge sheet for theft and some other less serious offences. The Sergeant rang the Manor House and spoke to Jake. After the call he looked like a man who had just lost a day's winnings on the last race as he said with reluctance, 'You are fortunate. Mr Paddington, the farm manager, said he lent you the tractor, but you might not remember. He is organizing a local recovery service to pick up you and the tractor and take you back to the farm. He has promised to put the other matters right and not to lend you any more vehicles for joyriding.'

I was frustrated and disappointed. I seemed to be likely to get to London, and now I was going to be taken back to where I started from, an empty house at Willowpit Farm. I did feel Jake had been kind to me, but felt the police had ruined my hopes for the day. Why didn't they stop some other tractor? Come to think of it, I hadn't seen another one for the whole of the journey. I definitely decided that a minority of one deserves to be left alone.

A lowloader with a sullen bearded driver, the red tractor plus oil leak and myself were quickly organized. We headed with more speed than I had become used to towards Norfolk. The driver, with his black oily hands gripping the wheel, said nothing and kept his eyes on the road. He looked to me exactly like Sam's double. He wore a jumble of filthy old clothes which were topped by a silent head of wild brown bushy hair. After an hour of total silence I was convinced that I was sitting next to Sam. Instinctively, I said quietly, 'Do you still want a gun?'

The driver glanced at me, looked back at the road, just missed a cyclist and said in an alarmed voice, 'What did you say?'

The voice and the briefly seen facial expression told me clearly that I'd got the wrong man. 'Do you want some gum?' I said, trying to sound repetitive.

'No, filthy stuff,' came the welcome reply.

Just as well, I thought, as I hadn't got any, and if I had would probably have swallowed it all whole and unchewed by now, as I was so hungry.

Nearing our destination, I made a last attempt to have a conversation with the driver.

'Do you pick up many tractors?'

'Yes, but this is the first one off the main road to London!' he said, tightly closing the moist partially-obscured gap between moustache and beard when he had finished his sentence, implying he preferred it that way.

2.

It was six o'clock in the evening, and I was desperate for something to eat and drink. I went straight to the fridge. To my amazement and delight, it contained a wide selection of food that I particularly liked. While I was looking and deciding what I was going to eat, I consumed a pork pie and a bottle of milk as a starter.

I found my armchair in the sitting room and made myself comfortable with an enormous selection of pate, fruit and toast on a tray on my lap. The owls seemed to be eyeing my food, but they did not deter me from eating. I decided to propel the little blighters out of the window into the night where they belonged as soon as I had finished my meal.

I was gradually feeling relaxed and wondering why Clare, who seemed to dislike me so much last night, should have left me with a larder full of wonderful food.

There was a knock at the front door, and in walked Clare, looking cheerful but businesslike. She flicked some of her dark hair slightly away from one side of her face, which when revealed was seen to be elegant and made up with the precision of an expert sign writer. Her little black pencilled eyebrows always intrigued me because I'd never seen her do any hair plucking, and I didn't believe she was born without any eyebrows. I could see nothing about Clare that was out of place as she carefully sat down on the settee. She seemed to be behaving very much as though she was a visitor in my house, which made me feel awkward because I certainly did not feel like the host in his home.

'Michael, Jake has paid off the lorry driver and the tractor is back in the barn,' Clare said, giving me a slight and definitely unexpected smile.

'Thank you,' I said, 'and for the food.' I was still wondering why the traumas of last night were not mentioned and why she hadn't taken up a fresh verbal attack on me after my strange behaviour today. Perhaps she had been totally distracted by Jake's well-hidden charm. Unlikely, I thought.

'Michael, Jake and I have been talking,' said Clare while I kept quiet but interested. 'We knew you had gone off today by midday, because Don found the plough when he came looking for you. This is the second day in succession that you have gone off in the same direction. Where are you trying to get to?' she asked earnestly. There was a pause as she took a dainty white handkerchief out of her handbag. It was so small that I decided anyone with a slightly bigger nose would have found it useless. 'We will help you get there,' said Clare, after a gentle wipe of her nose which can't have even disturbed her layer of fine powder. That really did sound a good idea, I thought excitedly.

'Very well,' I said, 'I'll tell you. I am trying to get to a flat in Eaton Square in London. That is where my friend is. The one I told you about last night.'

'What's her name? Did you meet her in hospital?' said Clare in a very direct manner.

'She is Mary-Anne, and yes, we met at the hospital.'

Clare looked obviously pleased with her questioning, but she asked, 'So you love her so much that you feel little for other women, including me?'

'Of course I like you, Clare, particularly as you are David's mother, but what you say about other women is true,' I said as my real feelings about Mary-Anne came rushing to the surface in front of Clare for the first time. 'Inside myself I'm obsessed by the need to be with her for every moment of every day. You can throw what you like at me, but it won't change a thing. More than anything else I need to share my very being, my very existence, in the vital, electric, loving company of Mary-Anne. She is the only person who makes me look forward to another day and enables me to feel that my life can be enjoyed. The doctor's pills and potions are no substitute for sharing in the magic that Mary-Anne possesses.' I paused, and then pleaded with damp eyes and clasped concerned hands, 'Will you really help me to find her?'

'You've really got it bad!' said Clare, looking surprised and slightly amused. 'I had no idea,' she said. 'Is she wealthy?'

'I have no idea, and don't care!' I said abruptly. I knew Clare wouldn't understand. How could she? I asked myself. She had never met Mary-Anne or seen what a different person I was when we were together. A special friend to Clare basically had to provide money and sex. What about the uplifting joy of togetherness that changes the quality of lives when two people can live inside each other's minds and hearts? I do not know what you are talking about, would certainly be her honest reply.

'Will you help me to find her?' I repeated to Clare in a louder, more desperate voice.

'Yes I will, now that I've got Jake,' she said with casual condescension. At that moment Jake walked noisily into the room, wearing his jodhpur boots with metal plates on the heels. He sported his tweed jacket and moleskin trousers. A country gentleman in the making maybe, but I thought he had a long way to go before he looked convincing, particularly as he still had mud-engrained hands.

'Hi Michael,' was mumbled as he dropped his huge body into the remaining armchair. 'You know, Clare and I will be getting married just as soon as your divorce can he arranged,' he said without a flicker of feeling.

I replied, 'I guessed as much. I hope you will be very happy.'

'We will,' he said, looking at the opposite wall.

Turning to look at Jake, Clare said with pleasure, 'Michael has got a mistress in London.'

'Good,' he said.

'No, she's not my mistress,' I said emphatically, 'she is everything.' Two blank faces indicated that I had made another misunderstood statement.

'As you wish,' said Jake, not caring what sort of girlfriend I had, as long as I had one to help divorce proceedings. 'So you won't want this house or . . .'

I interrupted Jake and said, 'Or anything.' I felt quite incapable of being practical about housing, money, jobs or anything else at the moment. I believed that when the time came, if there was something Mary-Anne wanted, I would have the renewed strength and energy to be able to get it for her.

Jake sat up in his chair, leant forward and rested his elbows on his knees. He looked purposeful as he said, 'Right, as Clare has probably told you, we don't want you living next door to us or crashing our cars or damaging tractors. So between now and the inevitable decree nisi we will help you to make a permanent home elsewhere with your new lady. Tomorrow Clare will get you some money and take you to the local station.'

Clare spoke out and explained a point Jake would not have considered. 'Oh, by the way, a Doctor Ogilvey has got your hospital notes. He's a consultant psychiatrist in Diss. If you need to see him, I can always take you to him before going to London. He is supposed to be very good.' She tried to catch Jake's eyes and said earnestly, 'Jake, do you remember Mrs Sadler who had an obsession about washing herself all the time?'

Jake laughed and said without sympathy, 'She must have been the cleanest woman in Britain. I'm surprised she had any skin left.'

'Well,' said Clare, composing herself, 'Doctor Ogilvey cured her. She is now a swimming pool attendant.'

'I bet she brings a bar of soap to work and jumps in the

pool for a good scrub,' contributed Jake in his customary carefree humour.

They both looked at me keenly, waiting anxiously for my reply. 'Well, I will definitely take you up on your offer to help me get to London, but I'll see Dr Ogilvey only when I really need to, perhaps on some other occasion,' I said, knowing that what I wanted to do happened to fit in well with their plans to have me living as far away from their Manor House as possible.

'Right, we will pack you off in the morning,' said Jake as he stood up. He clearly wanted this meeting to close, now that what he had wanted seemed to have been agreed to.

'You will look after David?' I asked both of them with some concern.

'Of course,' they said in unison. Jake then said, 'Jessie will help. I am weaning her off the booze, you know.' I knew I had my doubts about that situation, but Clare made a more sympathetic remark.

'You will be able to come and see him from time to time. It would be wrong for him to lose touch completely with his real father.'

Jake found that the extended conversation was irritating him, and told Clare firmly, 'It is time to go.'

'Coming, darling,' Clare said obediently. A moment later she called from the front door, 'I will see you in the morning, Michael. I should do some packing tonight.'

I opened the window and threw the owls with their painted dilated pupils into the darkness where they belonged. I then went to bed, feeling that at last tomorrow would bring me my Mary-Anne and an end to my frustration and loneliness at not being understood.

The bright spring morning saw me up early with a large well-packed suitcase and a strong feeling of excitement running through my body.

Clare duly arrived, wearing a heavily flowered brown and orange cotton dress, which I felt pleased to be leaving behind. She then gave me a new chequebook and said, 'There is a thousand pounds in your account, and here,' giving me a brown envelope, it's two hundred pounds in cash. Keep it safe. Did you have any breakfast?'

'Yes, thank you,' I replied, 'I raided the fridge and did very well.'

'Michael,' she said, looking at my open-neck shirt, 'I should wear your jacket and tie. London is a smart place, you know.'

When Clare considered I was appropriately dressed for the city, she and I set off in Jake's Land Rover. I realized that I hadn't said goodbye to David. I consoled myself with the thought that I would see him again soon, and that he was probably playing happily with Jessie.

My chauffeur and guide continued with her very direct instructions. 'You change trains at Ipswich and then at Liverpool Street Station, I should take a taxi to the flat, or you're bound to get lost.' I felt that, in spite of Clare saying to me the other night, 'I never want to see you again,' she still seemed to care what happened to me.

At the station I gave Clare a formal peck with my lips on the side of her face and then, displaying a slightly cautious smile, said, 'Good luck with Jake,' and boarded the train.

The journey was surprisingly easy with no steering for me to do, and with no traffic, including roadsweepers, for me to worry about. After one confusing change of trains I eventually arrived at Liverpool Street Station in the heart of London. I was very excited, and as most people in my carriage were pushing and shoving to get out of one side door, I decided to open the vacant door on the other side of the train. The result was that I nearly walked into space with a painful six-foot drop to the rails below.

No-one had noticed my mistake as they were too concerned about 'politely' fighting their way onto the platform. Anyone would think that the train was on fire! I thought the enthusiasm of all the passengers to get to their chosen destinations matched mine, but they were conditioned to the hazards of their regular journey and I wasn't.

I followed behind rows of fast moving legs while tilting my body sideways to try to counter the weight of my suitcase. As I walked and looked around I thought that this must be one of the most impersonal, non-caring places in the entire world. If some poor chap was to fall over, I was sure he would be trampled to death by misguided feet. 'Darling, one of your stiletto heels has a little blood on it. Have you got a tissue?' one husband might casually say later to his wife.

I found myself in the taxi queue, having had to read a dozen other signs first, including being invited to have a haircut below ground level in the Gents!

It was my turn at last. I instructed a black cabby with contrasting grey moustache to please take me to one hundred and thirty-five Eaton Square.

'Okay, man,' he said as he put my suitcase beside him and opened the door at the back with a well-practised unsighted backward reach of his right arm from his driving position.

Before I had time to sit comfortably, we were charging into a mayhem of traffic. I had no idea of our route or how long it would take or exactly when we were going to have an accident. I found travelling by taxi was made easier by totally ignoring what the driver was doing. I stared at the roof of the cab and tried to let my mind wander to almost anywhere that did not include noisy bumper car traffic, crowded pavements, negative expressions and the rear view of my driver's head.

The taxi suddenly stopped outside one of a row of large houses that all had white-pillared porches outside their smart front doors. 'Here you are, man,' the driver said, repeating his backward reaching exercise to allow me out on to the welcome pavement. Suitcase in hand and cabby paid, I started to get nervous shakes in my hands and knees as I began to climb the steps past the number one hundred and thirty-five painted in black on the pillar. To the left of the black front door was a list of names. I looked carefully at the list and quickly saw in disbelief, Flat C: Miss M. Cheyney. 'My God, I've found the right one!' I said quietly but excitedly. As I pressed the appropriate little button with my tremoring finger, worrying thoughts raced through my head. What was I going to say to her? Did she need me as much as I needed her? What do I do if she tells me to go away? I knew if she did reject me after all this time I would be finished as a human being. It seemed a straightforward but terrifying situation.

Softly and calmly, Mary-Anne's voice spoke to me. 'Who is it?'

'It's Michael, Michael Simpson,' I replied eagerly.

'Come up two flights of stairs and I will be waiting for you,' she said, gently and without any fuss.

'I'm on my way,' I said. I could not wait a moment longer to see her. I left my case at the bottom of the stairs and then ran up two flights with the ample strength and speed that my forgotten nerves now allowed.

There was Mary-Anne standing waiting for me, but at first glance she seemed different. She appeared to have changed in some way. She let me hold her, but only encouraged a small kiss on the cheek.

She took me politely into the better light of the flat, where I could not believe my eyes. She was dressed in a humble drab brown knitted sweater, a long dark grey skirt and flat shoes. She had also put on weight, and looked podgy in the face, with signs of an extra chin. The lovely shiny curly blonde hair that I remembered and liked so much was now dull and almost straight.

'Do sit down, Michael. Would you like tea and biscuits?' she said quite kindly, with a pale and almost bored facial expression. I could not believe my ears. Mary-Anne, after all this time, seemed to be treating me like a casual visitor.

'Yes please,' I said, feeling very confused.

The tea came in a very organized way in a matching china tea service. I could not help noticing that all the biscuits were of the same plain type. This is ridiculous, I thought. Mary-Anne would normally have chosen fancy ones with holes in them or in funny shapes.

Mary-Anne sat on the sofa beside me and started to talk to me like a superficial acquaintance. I looked at her eyes. They were still blue, but a sad blue. Her sparkle, her magic, her *joie de vivre*, and her moments of hysterical laughter had all gone. She seemed just another boringly sensible person who takes life as they find it and always obeys the rules.

Mary-Anne told me that she now had a job as a secretary to a firm of house agents. On Sundays she said that she went to church, and particularly enjoyed hymn singing. I thought that beautiful operatic voice should be heard solo.

145

I also thought that if she did not at least smile soon I would be forced to tickle her out of desperation.

I wanted her to giggle, to tease me and importantly to behave in that carefree manner that meant my desire to love and protect her could be fulfilled.

Inside myself I was heartbroken, and did not know what to say or do. She must change back to the lively exciting person that I lived for. I remembered her bubbly moments of mania that used to lift me from the depths of despair into a feeling of sheer delight and pleasure for my existence. These moments seemed to have gone for ever. I found this very ordinary, run of the mill, over-polite, limp lady unattractive. However, I believed and needed to believe that the lady I knew and bled for could exist again. I did not accept that my Mary-Anne was dead and gone forever. I knew that for the sake of both our lives she simply couldn't be!

I was terribly upset and near to tears. I brought up my suitcase and asked, 'Mary-Anne, may I stay with you for a few days?'

'Yes,' she said, raising her head into an inquiring receptionist's pose. 'It's so nice to see you, Michael. You are more than welcome to have the spare room.'

Me in the spare room, I thought, somewhat taken aback! Although I knew her magical attractiveness had left her and that under these circumstances I would have felt awkward and barely capable of sleeping with her, I was still surprised that there was no offer at least to share her room. In the past I remembered a golf course and a Mini car were acceptable to her for lovemaking. Now a comfortable bed was available, she would not suggest using it!

10

1.

We spent a quiet evening telling each other about our lives since we left St Matthews. Mary-Anne looked very tired, so she went to the bathroom to take her medications and prepare for a good night's sleep. As she walked back into the sitting room to get to her bedroom she gave me a gentle wave and then retired to bed.

I took the opportunity to see from the display of brown bottles in the mellow green fitted bathroom what pills Mary-Anne was taking. On the glass shelf just below the mirror I found strong night sleeping pills, lighter daytime sedatives and, to my surprise, a bottle of carbonate salt tablets. I stood back with amazement. She was on the same parallel line treatment as myself, but for different reasons! It seemed no wonder to me that, with all her sedation, Mary-Anne looked dull, drowsy and no longer was my confident, chuckling, teasing, unrestrained laughing girl. I decided that I must encourage her in the morning to stop taking her pills and I would stop mine. Indeed, I would hide hers. If she couldn't sleep at night, she would have to get help from me or a whisky bottle.

I lay on my small, adequate bed and continued to think about Mary-Anne, who was sweetly asleep in the room next door. As I saw the situation, we were both wandering about in the uncomfortable mist of normal acceptance mood levels. I knew that if she was back above the lines and I was sagging below, our attraction for each other would return to its previous enormous strength. Then I thought that, provided we were together, we would pull ourselves painlessly in life's demanding required directions. We would still have time to take each other into our little understood and private world of togetherness that could, I believed, be so close that it might be compared with the unity demanded of a pulsating heart within a living body.

The next morning I was woken by the sound of Mary-Anne getting dressed. I jumped out of bed. Wearing just my pyjamas, I knocked on her bedroom door and walked straight in. Mary-Anne was dressed in a plain white blouse and a long dark grey suit. She looked dowdy, drab and uniformed for her office job.

'Good morning, Michael,' she said, 'I've got to walk to work soon. I can't find my pills in the bathroom. I'll never cope without them. Have you seen them?'

'Yes, my poor love, I've hidden them. I must talk to you,' I said, worried by the look of alarm on her face.

'Hidden them!' she exclaimed. 'I've got to go to work or I will be in trouble for being late.'

I tried my utmost to be masterful and said toughly, 'I will ring your boss and get you some time off.' Mary-Anne looked confused and did not reply. I went up to her and held her tightly to me. I gently stroked the back of her neck and let my fingers play with her dull, straight hair.

'All right,' she said softly, 'you are rather special and I don't often see you. Actually, I don't often see anybody.'

I rang her office. I spoke to the manager and explained that I was Miss Cheyney's doctor. I said that I regretted that she was unfit to work for at least a week due to severe rigidity of her usual cyclothymic movements. Confused but helpful came the reply, 'Well, I am sorry. She is owed two weeks holiday from last year. Do you think she should take that?'

'Definitely. Thank you,' I said quickly. 'My patient needs the rest.'

I turned to Mary-Anne, who was also standing near the telephone in the sitting room, and said, 'You are now free from work worries, so let's talk about other things.'

'Where are my pills, Michael? I must have my pills!' she said a little crossly.

'Sit down,' I said gently, finding an edge of the sofa for myself near to her. 'My love, you don't need to be made drowsy during the day. Please believe me.'

148

'You take pills,' she retorted.

'Yes, you're right,' I said peaceably. 'Indeed, I have taken pills for so long now that I'm not at all sure whether I still need them or not. Who is the real Michael Simpson? The same is true for you. Wouldn't it be worth finding our natural unmedicated selves again?'

'If you put it like that, I suppose it would be fun. I don't really enjoy my present way of life,' she said, sounding a little uncertain.

I stood up and took Mary-Anne by the arm and led her to the bathroom, saying, 'I'll tell you, my love, what we will do. We will throw away our pills together.'

'Are you absolutely sure you know what you're doing, Michael?'

'Yes,' I said firmly.

We opened each pot of pills in turn, including the ones I had hidden, and tipped their contents into the water-filled toilet bowl. I dropped the empty pots and bottles into a white plastic pedal bin. I then looked into Mary-Anne's worried face and gently squeezed her soft hands in an attempt to reassure her. After a moment I turned to the green cistern and flushed the toilet.

'There,' I said, looking down at the rush of water, 'they are gone for ever. We can now get back to being ourselves. You will soon become the real, unsedated, happy Mary-Anne!' Then I thought of the girl I remembered and loved so passionately and knew I would again. I looked closely at Mary-Anne, my poor and subdued love, and reassured myself that my plan had got to work. We kissed each other gently but meaningfully on the lips.

'I hope you are right,' whispered Mary-Anne with the indication of a smile.

During the morning I was pleased to notice that Mary-Anne was less sleepy, more alert and more talkative than she had been the day before. 'Let's brighten up your flat,' I said eagerly.

'Why not? What do you want me to do?' Mary-Anne asked.

'Well, I'll order some flowers to be delivered. We can both put some of the dusty old photographs and that crucifix on the wall up there into a cupboard. We will

149

polish up the furniture and put up in the bathroom some of your brightly coloured posters that I noticed in the sideboard.'

Near to lunchtime the flat looked a little more cheerful. Mary-Anne definitely seemed to have extra energy, and prepared omelettes with an 'anything can go in them' filling. We sat opposite each other with our plates of food on our laps. We were both looking pleased with ourselves.

In between forked mouthfuls of 'eggy plus' food, Mary-Anne confessed, 'I used to have some good times, very good times, but the police were always arresting me.'

'This could happen again,' I warned, 'but to save that happening, I want us to both go "home" well before our behaviour becomes unacceptable and causes problems. I want us to be together back in our safe place and away from the painful confusion of this hazardous outside world existence.' I looked anxiously for her reaction to my strongly-meant words.

'You mean St Matthews?' she asked softly, while appearing to be looking at some distant object through the window behind me.

'Yes,' I said, 'St Matthews; you will remember it was there that we had some of our best times together.'

Mary-Anne moved her head slightly, enabling her to look straight at my eyes. 'You had better keep away from the padded cells,' she said with concern.

'That won't happen again,' I said reassuringly. 'It was a mistake by officials last time. Now I know how their minds work.'

I felt very pleased with the way Mary-Anne had taken my suggestions. I decided it was the right time to continue. I placed my clean plate on the floor and leant back into the soft armchair. 'Mary-Anne, as you know I have let go of my wife and son. Now I have no family. My entire world revolves around you. I love you now, but I know my feelings towards you will get even stronger as you gradually become your adorable natural self again. You will enjoy life so much more, and we will take immense pleasure from doing everything we can together.'

Mary-Anne pushed her plate on to a gold coloured cushion, and then, without speaking, came over to me and sat sideways on my lap. She put an arm affectionately round my neck. Her seemingly imminent verbal reaction to what I had just said distracted me from the fact that she was heavy and her bottom was squashing my thighs.

'Michael,' she said very clearly and definitely, while she was also so close to me that I could feel her warm breath on the side of my face, 'I need you too. You are my family and friends all rolled into one. I thought that I would be trapped as a boring, lonely "battery hen" for the rest of my life. Now, with you, I see a chance for my old enjoyable freedom to return. I've always wanted you to be mine from the first moment I met you. I was held back by the thought that one day you would want to return to live with your wife and son. I expected you to forget all about me. Now I know that we are truly together, my life takes on a new and exciting meaning.'

Mary-Anne's tights-covered legs were hanging over the edge of my chair. Her words and her warmth were making me feel wonderful. My plan was going to be, as I had hoped, of mutual benefit for the rest of our lives. I put my hand on her knee and stroked it gently. 'Darling,' I said, 'tell me all you are thinking.'

'Well,' she said, 'I know that if, as I expect, I soon become over-elated once more, which I've really missed not being able to do, the best place for me to be is back in hospital, provided, of course, you are there. I want to be re-admitted before there is any risk of me causing an accident or ending up in a police cell for something silly.'

She put her other arm round me and pulled us even closer together. 'Michael,' she said, looking very serious for a moment. 'I need you to share my moments of great elation and being high.'

'Equally, my love,' I said, unconsciously playing with her left ear, pressing it gently between my fingers, 'I need your flow of happiness and laughter to desolve my often persistent private morbid thoughts and give me a worthwhile reason for living. I don't need to be drugged by well-meaning doctors. I need to be left alone with the freedom to be allowed to be infatuated by you, when you also have been allowed to be free from the unfortunate too-human intrusion on the lives of their fellow beings in order to

151

bring them into line.

'Mary-Anne, stand up, my darling,' I said, giving her large, soft bottom a little assistance with my hands.

Mary-Anne stood tall and proud in front of me with a tender, pleased expression on her face. My thigh muscles still did as they were told, if a little stiffly, but they enabled me to stand up in front of her. We looked without moving for several moments into the depths of each other's eyes. Suddenly neither of us could wait any longer. We threw our arms around each other, our lips, mouths and tongues together.

After a timeless embrace I let my arms' firm hold on her lose their strength. She spoke to me quietly.

'Michael, darling, we need to help each other to get back to the hospital, and we will never stop needing each other when we get there. I have always loved you deep inside myself, but when I'm elated I express myself rather light-heartedly.'

'I know, my love,' I said, smiling at her. 'Do you think the hospital will do married quarters for us?'

She held me tighter and then giggled for the first time that I could remember since leaving St Matthews.

During the afternoon we lounged about listening to music and drinking cans of beer from Mary-Anne's extraordinarily large stock. We were both going through the process of learning to relax without the aid of prescribed sedatives.

Time sped by, and we were soon hungry again. 'Do you like pizzas?' asked Mary-Anne.

'I'm not sure that I've ever eaten one,' I said.

'Well, try one,' she said. 'I will order two from the Pizza House, which will save us having to go out.' She then quickly used the phone and then announced, 'I'm going to put on my pretty black dress that you like so much.'

Overdressed in her black and blonde attempt at past splendour, and me now looking shabby by contrast, we started to eat our newly-arrived burning hot pizzas off a small coffee table placed between the sofa and my armchair. I had found a whisky bottle and had given us both a 'double double' because I was worried we were going to find it difficult to sleep that night.

As I fought to cut off a piece of pastry with un-identifiable topping about the right size for my mouth, I glanced up at Mary-Anne and said, 'Have you got your own doctor in London?'

'Yes,' she said, with a partially full mouth, 'he lives in the Square. He is the man who admitted me last time.'

'Good,' I said, 'don't for heaven's sake tell him you have stopped your pills. He probably won't ask, particularly if you ask for your monthly repeat prescription when you normally would.' I put down my knife and fork and drank a large gulp of neat whisky. I now felt more able to continue.

'My love, if you get to the stage of wanting to rob the Bank of England accompanied by the brass band of the Metropolitan Police Force . . .' I stopped. I could see from her face that she was worried by my exaggerated example, so I said, 'I'm sorry, but you know what I mean. If you feel things are getting out of control, you must ring your doctor straight away.'

'Why, where will you be?' she said, looking most concerned.

'Well, I've got to go tomorrow to try to convince my doctor, Doctor Ogilvey from Diss, that I should be re-admitted to St Matthews. With luck, we may be apart for only a couple of weeks. Then, my love, we will be partners for life in our protected "home."'

'Until they make us conform,' she said intelligently.

'I've thought of that,' I said. 'If we both refuse tablets, they would not force-feed us, and they can't evict us if we are not fit enough to be put in the world outside. I'm not worried.' I took a breath and said, 'Anyway, whenever or wherever we go, we will stay together once we have got back "home". We will always provide each other with the caring treatment that we both really need.'

That night the two of us tried to find sleep in our separate beds. Neither of us was feeling in the mood for sex, but both of us knew that such events were not far away. I thought that I must have drunk half a bottle of Scotch, and Mary-Anne nearly the same.

I thought about Mary-Anne lying on the bed in the room next door. I found her more attractive than when I arrived, but she was still not quite my one and only exciting, vibrant, magical dream girl who gave me a reason for getting out of bed in the morning, indeed for living. I prayed that her wild happiness and unabashed confidence would soon return. I needed the sparkling uninhibited girl I loved so much. I reflected further, and decided that I had not done very well in the outside world. I thought, however, the future should give me freedom and happiness, without undue hazards and medications, in the only way I found effective.

I climbed out of bed, and in my pyjamas and bare feet I walked round to Mary-Anne's room. I looked in through her half open door, as a mother might have had a last 'goodnight' look at her child. She was sleeping sweetly and peacefully, which made me feel pleased as I returned quietly to my room to try and achieve the same state of rest.

In the morning, probably out of habit, Mary-Anne was up early and noisily preparing herself for a new day in the room next door.

It was not long before I joined her by the small kitchen table for what appeared to be a cereal and coffee breakfast.

'Did you sleep well?' I asked, confident that she had done.

'Yes, surprisingly well,' she said. Then she asked with a slightly wicked smile on her face. 'What are we going to do today?'

I was worried by her question. I thought I told her yesterday that I had to leave. 'Mary-Anne,' I said gently, 'I'm afraid I have to go today. Don't you remember?'

'Yes,' she said reluctantly, 'I just hoped that you had changed your mind.' While talking, she was attacking the toaster with a knife. A burnt piece had evidently got stuck.

'I was very sorry to read of your father's death,' I said, wishing I had left the remark until later in the day. 'By the way, I should unplug that toaster,' I said, with the help of belated observation.

Unperturbed, Mary-Anne said, 'Yes, his sister and I are all that are left of his family. My Auntie Helen lives in the next flat.'

Thinking quickly, I said, 'Would she keep an eye on you in case you need help?'

'She does already,' she said calmly. 'She pops in nearly every day, but remember she's nearly seventy. You don't have to worry, she rings the doctor if I so much as sneeze!'

'Marvellous,' I said, feeling slightly reassured.

There was now black ash all over the side, but Mary-Anne looked triumphant as she put some fresh bread into the toaster. 'Have you got a train timetable?' I asked hopefully. It was immediately handed to me, with secretarial efficiency, from the drawer beside her.

I rang Clare, who seemed surprised to hear from me. I asked her to get me an appointment with Doctor Ogilvey and to pick me up later from the station. She agreed and commented that David was learning to read and to rear pheasants, which seemed a rather strange combination to me.

I was packed and ready to catch one of those traffic-ignoring taxis. Mary-Anne had a slightly nervous expression on her face but nevertheless we gave each other a warm parting hug and a long sensitive kiss.

'I will ring you every day,' she said emotionally as I started to descend the stairs.

I turned my head so that I could look once more into those kind, blue eyes and said very clearly, 'Yes please, every single day.'

2.

At Willowpit Farm, after my expectedly confusing journey, Clare very willingly brought me a bacon sandwich and a mug of coffee. She then placed herself on the settee near to me, clearly waiting anxiously for a fuller report on my future plans than I had managed in her car. I felt Jake would also be keen to know when I was going to leave his 'patch' permanently.

I knew I was not answering the questions on her mind when I said, 'When can I see the doctor?'

'Tomorrow morning, and I'll take you,' she said, probably feeling curious about my priorities.

'Good,' I said.

'Don't you feel well?' she inquired with a tone of disbelief.

To save complicated explanations that would certainly not be understood by Clare, I said, 'No, terrible.'

'I see,' she said, not seeing at all, 'but you look quite well to me.' She then turned to look towards the fireplace and then returned to focus her small, piercing-eyed expression on me. Slowly and accusingly she said, 'You will be pleased to know that I picked up my owls off the drive and pieced them together back at the Manor.'

'Yes,' I said, 'it is difficult to keep night birds captive. They were probably after a nice feast of manorial mice.'

Clare, with her mouth slightly open, was looking at me with an expression that was saying, 'Michael, you are completely mad.' I knew, however, that Clare, poor thing, never had managed to find a sense of humour.

I was still muddled in my mind about my future plans as Clare wished me 'goodnight'. She left, no doubt, to get back and discuss the strange phenomenon of her separated husband with her 'real man', Jake, the more than ample physical being.

A little later the phone started to ring. I went quickly to answer it, hoping it was Mary-Anne. 'Hullo,' I said, helpfully I thought.

'Can I speak to Clare?' said a confident female voice.

'No,' I said firmly, wishing I was speaking to Mary-Anne. 'She's gone.'

'Oh, I am sorry, I didn't know,' she said, sounding concerned and misunderstanding the situation.

'Don't be sorry. I'm not,' I said cheerfully. 'If you ring Jake Paddington you will get her, if she's not too busy.'

'Thank you,' said a fading and confused voice.

I had just sat down when a second phone call turned out to be the one I wanted. Mary-Anne sounded chirpy and fairly sensible. 'I've been out and bought a new red dress and had my hair done. I'm very pleased with my day, but I desperately wish I could see you.'

'You can, my love, very soon. I hate being away from you, but it is necessary just for a short time,' I said regretfully.

156

'I miss you terribly, and I can tell you that if you were here now there would be no separate bedrooms for us tonight!' she said excitedly.

'We won't have to wait much longer before we are safely together. We are going to be able to make love together and do everything together whenever we want to,' I said to try to reassure her and added, 'I see the doctor tomorrow, so keep your fingers crossed for me.'

'I will,' she said. 'I will ring in the evening. I can't stand being away from you much longer. Bye.'

That night I lay in bed and thought tenderly about Mary-Anne. I missed her so much. I was still worried that my plan might not work. She must change back to the unfettered, joyful, bubbling beauty that I needed more than anything else in this life to make my existence worthy of the every day effort required to contribute and survive. As I closed my eyes to encourage sleep, I consoled myself with the thought that Mary-Anne seemed much happier since my visit to her flat. Progress was being made, I felt.

The next morning I rose late and had to scamper through the dressing process. I had already decided not to shave, to help my appearance to look uncared for. I didn't bother to wash or to knot my shoelaces. I grabbed an apple for a possible breakfast and dropped it in the pocket of my jacket.

I was then on parade, standing next to the newly-hammered, twisted and painted 'as good as new' body of Daddy's cherished Wolseley. Immaculately dressed, with her carefully created made up face done to perfection, Clare said, in a thoroughly disgusted voice, 'Michael, surely you are not going to see the doctor dressed like that? It is positively rude of you.'

'Clare,' I said in my 'for heaven's sake be reasonable' manner, 'he is only interested in my mind. I told you I was not well. People who are not well often look a mess.'

Clare displayed her annoyance at my total lack of pride in my appearance all the way from Willowpit Farm to the waiting room in the doctor's surgery. She avoided looking at me, and did not attempt to speak.

Doctor Ogilvey appeared a surprisingly young man to

be a medical consultant. I guessed that he was in his early thirties. He was dressed in a rag tie, red jersey and navy corduroy trousers. His appearance seemed little better than mine, but it seemed acceptable to me except for his blue plastic shoes with whitish corrugated rubber soles. I wondered if he used them for potholing. Indeed, I thought that he looked like a left-wing, shandy-drinking potholer.

'Well, Michael,' he said, 'what can I do for you?'

I foolishly, as it turned out, smiled politely before saying, 'I don't feel well. I think what I need is to be re-admitted to St Matthew's Hospital.

'Michael,' he said, 'your clothes are pretty scruffy and you haven't bothered to shave, but you seem alert and cheerful to me. I can't see a case for admitting you to St Matthews unless I considered you to be very ill or a danger to yourself or members of the public, and I don't!'

I was desperately worried that my plan was going all wrong. I thought about his last words, a 'danger to the public' he had said. I had an idea. I grasped the apple in my pocket and hurled it past the doctor at the surgery window. It hit the frame and bounced back on to the floor.

'Satisfied?' came a completely calm voice from Dr Ogilvey.

'No, I'm damn well not!' I said, picking up the apple and throwing it straight through a pane of glass. I felt satisfied then, with the hole in the window, broken glass on the carpet and the apple on the lawn. I turned to the doctor and said, in a rage, 'Well, what now?'

He looked most displeased and simply said, 'You owe me ten pounds for the repair. Make an appointment on your way out, hopefully on one of your less violent days!'

I was very subdued and felt unwilling to say much to Clare in the car during the return journey. I knew that I was in big trouble. Unless I came up with an effective solution to my problem, Mary-Anne would be at St Matthews without me, and all would be lost.

Clare said, seemingly unconcerned by my lack of conversation, 'I've got some shopping to do before we go home.'

'Fine,' I said, having given up caring about where we

158

were going.

The Wolseley slowed and parked at the edge of the curb near Drillingham's small shopping centre. Clare got out and started to walk purposefully up the High Street.

'I'm going to the butcher,' she called back. 'Somewhere you have never been,' she added with sarcasm.

I found myself left standing outside a 'fruit and veg' shop. My doctor's words, 'a danger to the public' were going through my mind as I looked through the busy shop window.

'Right,' I said to no-one in particular, and marched into the shop, past the cashier, to where bananas were hooked in bunches at eye level to the woodwork. I thought shoplifting was a crime and criminals were at least considered a danger to society, so why not try it? I lifted off their hook the largest group of fresh bananas that I could find. I walked back past other shoppers and the lady at the till. I displayed them in my hands in front of me. I found them quite heavy to carry, but so far my efforts had failed to attract any attention. You can't get caught until you leave the shop, my memory reminded me. So, in order to be outside and as obvious as possible, I leant with my back against the shop window. I then, with difficulty, held the bunch in one hand and ate a banana with the other. After about ten minutes and three bananas later, nobody had taken the slightest notice of me!

Clare approached the car with what I guessed was an armful of wrapped meat. 'Can you open the car door for me?' she shouted.

'Just a moment,' I yelled and ran back into the shop to hang up the now slightly lighter bunch of bananas, leaving three skins on the pavement. I tore off one more yellow handful before quickly dashing back to help Clare with her meat.

Seated back in the car I said to Clare, 'This is for you,' presenting her with my last illicit trophy.

'I don't like bananas,' she snapped at me. I wound down the window and threw it away. I simply couldn't eat another one, even if it was free pickings from my completely unobserved theft. I was upset by my failure and felt that my potential for criminal behaviour had a

159

great deal to be desired. I simply did not want to hurt anybody, or, for that matter, significantly damage other people's property. How therefore, I asked myself, was I going to get a ticket to go back 'inside'?

Clare dropped me off at her now obviously considered inferior past residence, where I stayed pacing round the ground floor and frustratedly talking to myself for the rest of the day. My major concern was that Mary-Anne could go manic and be admitted at any time in the near future. As for myself, there seemed no easy way for readmission, in spite of my pills having little if no effect on me by now. Turning to crime did not seem to be the answer for me. As well as going against my natural instincts, I knew that if I did anything too awful, and was considered to be in good health at the time, I might well not go to St Matthews but be sent to the cold confines of one of Her Majesty's prisons!

I remembered that I had, almost certainly against Doctor Ogilvey's better judgement, booked myself in to see him tomorrow. I knew for certain that I must not again resort to what he liked to call violence. After much thought, I decided that all there was left for me to try now was to fake my illness. Tired, limp, lethargic, unhappy, pathetic and suicidal seemed the ingredients that flooded to mind.

In the evening as I sat quietly on the sofa, I decided that for the best effect I would not go to bed that night. Then the phone rang and I quickly answered it. I put the receiver to my ear and could hear pop music. 'Hullo Mary-Anne,' I said expectantly.

'Yes, darling, it's me,' came a bubbling, slurred voice. 'I'm having a party with Auntie Helen. It's a swan and rabbit party!'

'Who's the rabbit?' I asked, feeling slightly surprised.

'Auntie, of course,' said Mary-Anne. 'I made her furry ears out of a piece of my fur coat. Mink ears – not bad! I'm afraid Auntie's a bit drunk. Well, she wouldn't come to the party at first. I'm trying to get some more guests. I've rung the Prime Minister, but he's not about. He is probably re-shuffling his cabinet or having a grapefruit juice and cream massage. I'm going to ring the Archbishop of

Canterbury. He might like to bless the swan of Eaton Square, but he'll have to come as a rabbit or his hat won't fit under the door.' She giggled merrily.

I thought Mary-Anne would never stop gibbering on. I felt, poor thing, she sounded as high as a kite and without anyone to share her feelings with.

'Mary-Anne,' I said, feeling very concerned. 'My love, ring your doctor and ask him to your party. Tell him to also come as a rabbit. How about as a pink one? I'm sure he likes parties.'

'OK, darling, I will ring him, then the Archbishop, and of course the Beatles and any people in the Square, or any square for that matter. Can you come, darling, please?'

'No, not tonight, my love,' I said immovably, in spite of being worried for her safety. 'Just remember to ring and invite your doctor. Invite his whole family if you like,' I insisted.

'Yes, I will,' she said clearly, and then continued to giggle.

I raised my voice and said, 'Can I speak to your legless Aunt?' After several moments of indiscernable background noises and no Aunt, I put the phone down and said, 'Glory, I don't believe it!' to an empty room. I expected something like this to happen sometime, but the form it had actually taken left me feeling surprised.

I fell back into the sofa and tried to relax and think. I believed there was a high chance that Mary-Anne would be admitted to St Matthew's tomorrow. I felt sad that we did not look like going 'home' together. However, I swore to myself that I was certainly not going to let her go there without me for a moment longer than I could avoid.

My determination to succeed with Doctor Ogilvey tomorrow hardened. I drank black coffee and watched television to the close of broadcasting. I then kept myself awake by walking and later staggering round the garden. I must have fallen asleep at some stage, because I was woken when lying flat out on the lawn by a sniff and a lick on the face from Tessa doing her early morning rounds.

Cold, damp and hungry, I returned to the house. I did nothing to smarten myself up, and didn't try to satisfy my appetite. I was sporting two days of neglected facial

161

stubble as I rang Clare and reminded her of my appointment.

I was just going out to the car when the phone rang. It was a lady calling herself Aunt Helen to say that her niece was taken in early this morning to St Matthew's.

She said, 'She probably thought I had too much to drink last night. Poor girl seemed to think everyone, including me, was drunk. She was very happy when she left, and asked me to ring you and to tell you she would see you soon.'

There was a pause before I said very softly, 'Thank you, Aunt Helen.'

I went out to the car feeling shattered and worried now that half my plan had worked, but was useless without the other half. As I got into the car I knew that I had the appearance of a discarded gypsy, and a very hungry one at that, but damn it, I didn't feel unwell.

I was racked with concern for Mary-Anne and myself. I knew that for both our sakes we simply had to be together. I felt sure that Dr Ogilvey would not begin to understand my argument.

We drove off as yesterday, with Clare again managing to lose her temper about my appearance. She almost refused to take me. She drove slowly and in silence, but no doubt her cross mind was keeping her occupied. I wound my window down to allow my tired face the pleasure of some fresh morning air.

We came up to some traffic lights just as they had changed to red. On the pavement near to me was an overweight mother dressed in drab clothes, pushing a pram with a baby in it. Beside the pram was an equally poorly-dressed little boy wearing only a grubby shirt and shorts, running to keep up. He looked about five years old. I thought he was about the same age as David. He had bright eyes, but there was evidence of a cold displayed by a sore, wet upper lip spreading up to his nose. He put out one hand and caught hold of the edge of the pram. His mother promptly yelled at him.

'I've told you before not to touch the bloody pram when I am pushing it!' She stopped walking and then, using all her ugly weight and strength, smacked the little boy with the palm of her hand full in the face. He cried and screamed. As the lights changed to amber then green I was hurt to see that she had left him to his misery and had walked on, pushing the future object of her cruel temper in her pram.

Poor little devil, I thought, putting my hand up to my eyes which had started to produce a few tears. After a further mile or two, I started to notice a tremor in my hands and my crying was profuse. Clare glanced off the road to look at me and said, 'Michael, what on earth is the matter?'

'I don't know,' I said, telling the absolute truth. I thought, somewhat alarmed, that I had tried to look ill and now, without explanation, I really was! I knew the small boy's pain had certainly upset me, but not to the point of helpless hysterical crying and the return of that old, intangible feeling of despair. I felt desperately that I needed my Mary-Anne now, this moment!

Doctor Ogilvey looked at my childlike crying, shaking figure and without hesitation rang St Matthew's and booked me in. Clare then used the doctor's phone to say to Jake that she would be late for lunch, without giving him a reason.

Clare kindly drove me to the hospital. During the journey I asked myself if I thought I was well enough to see Mary-Anne. I felt that in my present state I might upset her. Would I be able to stop crying and talk to her, I wondered? I simply did not know. My emotions for the time being seemed out of my control.

On arriving at St Matthew's, we were greeted by staff nurse Graham with a much longer head of hair and a less harsh appearance than I had remembered. As a pleasant surprise, he showed me to my old room that was so comfortingly familiar to me.

As I propped myself up on the edge of the bed, Clare bent over me and whispered, 'Graham tells me Mary-Anne is in the hospital somewhere. I'd love to meet her one day. She must be very special. Michael, I'll say goodbye now, and good luck.' Clare touched my face with her lips, then quietly turned and walked away.

'Cheer up, mate,' came an unmistakable voice through

my open door. I knew it was Jamie. He came in and put his arm round my shoulders. 'You will soon feel better. It's particularly nice to see you. I've been a bit lonely since they found me back on the smokes and made me come here again,' he said, with a caring smile.

In the early evening, I was distressed but much calmer. I looked at my rough appearance in the mirror and felt ashamed. I could see that my eyelids were red and sore from excessive crying.

'This is how I am. It's just too bad,' I said aloud to my reflection before I moved out of my door towards the main entrance. Graham and Jamie were talking together by the front door. On reaching them, I said to Graham in a soft voice, 'Where can I find Mary-Anne?'

'Michael, if you go down to the beech tree you may well find her there,' he said with a partially-disguised grin, as though he had a secret that he was finding difficult to keep.

'Thank you, I will,' I said rather breathlessly.

I encouraged my tired and unhappy body to saunter down the tarmac path towards the handsome tree. I noticed Graham and Jamie had followed me out of the hospital and were casually strolling some twenty yards behind me. I reached my goal, which was the soft green grass-surrounded trunk of the splendid beech. The sun was gently going down on this clear, bright spring evening. I noticed my followers had stopped to have a chat some distance away.

I could not see Mary-Anne, and as I waited I wondered if I ever would. Suddenly, I heard a giggle from behind the tree. I knew it was the one and only sound that could so clearly give away Mary-Anne's presence. Before I could even take an eager step, my adorable, smiling, tall and beautiful, curly-headed blonde that I loved so much, was slowly walking round the tree. Her loose white blouse, yellow cotton skirt and white high heel shoes seemed to be saying, 'I'm still here for you. Nothing has changed.'

'Darling,' I said softly as we walked into each other's arms. I felt immediately that my sadness had started to melt into the joy and pleasure of our love.

We kissed tenderly, our lips longing for still more of

each other. Then, silently but hand in hand, acting as one being, we started to walk gently across the grass of the familiar golf course.

As I walked, I could just hear from behind me on the tarmac path the voice of Graham speaking to Jamie. 'When those two are together, they believe they have got something to enhance their lives more powerful than anything this hospital has to offer.'

I smiled to myself, and felt completely certain that he was right.

As I held her hand in mine, I knew that in the misunderstood privacy of our hearts and minds we had both found in each other the only meaning there was to our lives.